EARTH ALERT!
AND OTHER SCIENCE FICTION TALES

EARTH ALERT!
AND OTHER SCIENCE FICTION TALES

Kris Neville

WILDSIDE PRESS

CONTENTS

EARTH ALERT!

I

When Julia (she pronounced the name without the "a" at the end) was twenty-four, she inherited $22,000 from an obscure uncle in California. After deducting taxes and administrative expenses, the California State Court ordered the money transferred to her bank account. It came to $20,247.50.

She had been working in a local book store. "I haven't the vaguest idea why it came to me," she told the curious and covertly envious customers. "I guess he just didn't know anybody else."

She was a small, slender girl. Her eyes were bright and enthusiastic, her open smile so friendly that it was infectious.

The first afternoon when the money was actually in the bank under her own name, her father asked, "Well, what are you going to do with it?" He was genuinely curious. He owned his own home and was about to retire on a pension. He felt uncomfortable in the face of $20,247.50 — for which he was not able even to imagine a use.

Julia said, "I haven't exactly made up my mind yet." She intended to shop around for a husband, but she did not say this. She thought it would sound very callous to say: I'm going to buy me a husband: I've always wanted one.

Julia gave two weeks notice at the book store. When the time was up, she took her last pay check and went to one of the modest dress shops and bought herself a conservative brown suit.

"You have a very nice figure," the clerk told her.

"Thank you." She studied him critically and then shook her head sadly. He wouldn't do.

I've got to be sure I get the right one, she thought. I'll know him when I see him, she reassured herself. It certainly isn't this one.

There ought, she thought, to be a lot of eligible bachelors in Hollywood. The movies ought to attract them.

Two days later, she walked down to the bank and instructed the teller to transfer $5,000 of her money to a checking account in her name at the Security First National Bank in Los Angeles.

She told her father she was going to take a little vacation.

"There's plenty of eligible bachelors here," he said.

"Why dad!" she exclaimed indignantly. "And anyway, none of them ever has asked me."

"God help the man you set your mind on, that's all I can say."

II

Out beyond the orbit of the moon, there was a huge, wheel-shaped space station. Its rapid spin pressed the equivalent of one Earth gravity against its broad, thick rim. Once when the distortion field failed, the Mt. Palomar telescope tracked it for the better part of an hour, but earth astronomers attributed the track either to an irregularity in the photographic plate or to some peculiarity in the atmosphere.

Near the hub where the gravity was weak, the nine aliens lived; in the two rim compartments lived the mutants. There were almost a thousand of the latter — both male and female — in the larger compartment; and fewer than thirty — all male — in the smaller one.

"Soon, now," the mutants told each other with growing excitement, "we shall go down and kill them."

The aliens stepped up the power in the larger of the two transmitters. "Our indoctrination is perfect," they reassured themselves. "The mutants will not get out of hand."

III

Julia bought a round trip ticket on the Greyhound Bus and carried her bag to the waiting room. A few minutes later the bus drew up outside, bringing with it the exciting travel-smell of hot rubber and gasoline. Most of the passengers climbed out to stretch in the winter sunlight.

"Fifteen minutes," the driver said.

Julia picked up her bag and carried it outside. She gave her ticket to the driver, who was standing by the door, smoking a cigarette. Half way back in the bus she found an empty seat. She hoisted the bag — standing on her tip toes — to the rack above and settled into the seat, primly rearranging her dress.

But she was unable to relax. She stared out the window; the building across the lot presented an uninteresting and windowless expanse of brick. She yawned nervously and surveyed the other passengers who were beginning to filter back.

The driver dropped heavily into his seat behind the wheel; he pulled the door closed, and the motor purred. He counted his passengers in the mirror.

Julia tightened her lips, and her face wrinkled into a stubborn little frown. Her finger tapped restlessly on her knee. She resolved to bring the husband back with her.

She could buy the Castle Place out on Mannor Street for $4,000. She would have $10,000 left to buy him — to make the down payment on, at least — Beck's Hardware Store. From that they would realize a steady and an adequate income. She would give Saturday teas for the society women and show her husband off — in a neat, double breasted suit — in church on Sunday. They would go to the movies twice a week; they would go to dancing once a month. They would have three children, two boys and a girl. She would let her husband go moose hunting in Canada once a year, and weekends during bass season they'd go up to the lodge (I should be able to buy the Roger's cabin on Center Creek for a few hundred, she thought) and fish.

She suddenly wished she had flown to Hollywood. She was in a great hurry to get there, get the selecting over and done with, and get back.

At Joplin a young man got on and sat down beside her. She watched him, from time to time, out of the corner of her eye. Outside, the huge chat piles (said by the civic boosters to be the biggest in the world) paraded by the bus. Ought to start snowing again pretty soon, she thought. . . . It will be fun to swim in the Pacific in February.

After the bus crossed the Missouri–Kansas line she turned to the young man seated beside her. "I'm going to Hollywood," she said.

"Going to get in the movies?"

"Oh, no," Julia said, ". . . no." Her finger tapped impatiently on her knee.

"That's why most pretty girls go to Hollywood."

Julia blushed. Her eyes, brown and friendly, searched his face. "I'm the domestic sort," she said. "My name's Julia. What's yours?"

"My name's William."

"That's a nice name."

"Julia's a nice name, too."

"I majored in literature in high school," Julia said. "I like to read. I worked in a book store back home."

William shifted uncomfortably. "I don't read much."

Julia frowned. "I read a lot."

"Reading's all right."

"I like to curl up with a good book."

They fell silent.

Julia bit her lip, nipping it into redness with her white, even teeth. I guess I'm not much of a conversationalist, she thought. For a moment she felt tiny and afraid.

Dispiritedly she searched in her sandwich bag for an apple. She brought it out and regarded it intently.

"You want half?"

"No, thanks."

She found a pen knife in her hand bag and began to peel the apple, wrinkling her forehead in concentration.

The bus was in a state supervised section of the highway. It hit a chuck hole, and the pen knife slipped, slicing deeply into her finger. Annoyed and embarrassed, she watched the blood well up in the cut. She put the apple in her lap. "Oh, dear. . . ." She held the finger away from her.

William bent forward. "Euuuu," he said sympathetically. "Here. . . ." He reached for his handkerchief. But before the hand got to it, he reconsidered, perhaps remembering that handkerchiefs are unsanitary. "Euuuu," he said again, shuddering. He moved his hands helplessly and stared at the blood trickling from the finger onto the floor. "Euuuu."

Julia decided: No, he certainly won't do.

She glared angrily at her finger.

And the cut closed; the edges came together and joined in a neat, red line. The blood ceased to flow. The red line vanished as the flesh knitted. The finger was as scarless as it had been moments before.

"I'll be God damned," the young man said.

". . . that's very odd," Julia said. She held up the finger. She put the pen knife in her lap beside the apple and felt the finger.

"You must have some rare type of blood," William said.

She wiggled the finger. "You mean something like the reverse of hemophilia?"

"I don't guess I read enough to know big words: just some rare type of blood."

"Nothing like this ever happened before," Julia said, still watching the finger suspiciously. "I've never heard of anything like it."

Hello.

"Hello," she answered.

"What did you say?" the young man asked.

"I said, 'Hello'."

"*Hello.*"

"Didn't you say hello a moment ago?" Julia said, looking at him with an annoyed little frown on her face.

"No."

"No."

"That's funny. . . . "

Hello. Where are you?

"I'm right here beside you," she said.

"What are you talking about?" the young man said.

What planet are you on?

William's lips hadn't moved that time. She'd been watching. She thought the young man was somehow trying to make fun of her.

"Excuse me," she said coldly. She picked up her apple and her pen knife and her handbag and brushed past him into the aisle. She looked around, saw a seat three rows back on the opposite side of the bus. She went to it and settled down, moving over against the window.

William was staring around at her with a puzzled expression on his face.

Hello.

She jerked her head away from him angrily and stared out the window at the cold, barren plain. He's not at all nice, she thought.

Hello.

Grimly she refused to listen. He must be doing it with a sort of radio set, she thought. It's probably some sort of thing they advertize in magazines for $2.98. She blinked her eyes. I wish he'd stop. I don't think it's a bit funny.

Hello.

After a few more miles, the voice stopped.

Morosely Julia finished peeling her apple.

It was cold in the Hollywood bus depot; chill rain drizzled down from a leaden sky.

She stood in the protection of the building, bag in hand, shivering miserably. Twice she waved futilely for a cab. On the third attempt, she got one.

The driver opened the door for her, and she bolted through the rain to its inviting back seat.

"Take me to some nice hotel," she said.

The driver flipped up the flag and gunned the motor.

Five minutes later she was paying him ninety cents; leaving the extra dime out of the dollar for a tip, she ran for the hotel steps.

After she registered, she asked the fatherly old gentleman at the desk, "Where does a person go to meet people?" Water trickled down from her hair and across her face.

He bent forward and narrowed his eyes. "Meet people?" he asked; his tone had grown cold and suspicious.

She bit her lip in embarrassment. Did I say something wrong? she thought. "Never mind," she said, wanting to cry. "I'm not going to stay in this horrible town a minute more than I have to!"

"She," the bellboy said when he came down stairs, "is crazy."

"What do you mean?"

"You should have seen her walk through the door." He pronounced the last word emphatically.

"You mean door*way*."

"I mean door," the bell boy said. "It was closed when she done it."

"I'm going to have to keep an eye on her," the clerk said, clucking his tongue in dry disapproval.

Now how did I do that? Julia asked herself. She walked to the door and put her hand through it. She wiggled her fingers. She half-opened the door and put her hand through it again. It came out on the other side. She moved her arm back and forth. It felt prickly.

She crossed to the bed and sat down. This isn't so good, she thought. I've got to figure out how I did that.

She closed her eyes tightly. Other people can't put their hands through doors, she thought. Other people can't heal cuts by looking at them, either. . . . I never could before; I don't feel any different from other people.

And then a little chill of fear ran up and down her spine. Suppose the bed, the floor, the earth below were suddenly to become as unsubstantial as the door. I might drop clear through to China, to, to. . . .

Her fingernails were making red creases in her palms.

She stood up and stamped on the floor. Her knees trembled. The floor was solid.

She went to the door. It is solid, she thought. She let her fingers explore the surface. She sighed, feeling the rough texture of the wood.

Now, she thought. I can reach through it.

Her hand passed through it easily.

She went back to the bed and sat down.

I did it with my mind, she thought. I wanted to put my hand through the door, and I did. In front of the bell hop, I suddenly felt so sure that I could walk through the door that . . . I did.

I'm going to figure out how I did that, she thought, her mouth tightening into a thin little line of resolution. Because if I learned to do it, anyone else could learn. . . .

Hello.

Her hands clenched into annoyed little fists. She went to the window and looked out. She opened the door and looked up and down the corridor. No William.

Hello.

"He . . . hello."

Good, you can hear me. What planet are you on?

"The same planet everyone else is."

. . . the third one from the sun?

She tried to remember her high school science survey course; and she found that she could remember it very clearly. *Of course, it is.*

That's funny.

She realized that she had thought her last statement, and that he (she was sure that the voice belonged to a he) had answered it nevertheless. She was exchanging thoughts with someone!

Hello, she thought weakly. She gulped. *What do you look like? How many arms and legs do you have?*

Two of each.

Her mind was very alert and active. She could think with great clarity. *Describe yourself.* She received a mental impression of him.

She let out her breath. He was human, after all; as human as anybody. And handsome.

She laughed softly with relief: since he has never been able to find anyone like himself, he thought I was from another planet!

Eh?

Describe yourself again.

He complied.

Suddenly she knew with absolute certainty that this was the one she was looking for. Out of all the people on earth, here was a man made for her.

Could you put your hand through a wooden door?

Of course.

She smiled happily. She meant to have him.

Hello.

Hello.

There was silence.

She wrinkled her forehead and tapped her knee. He had ceased transmitting.

He'll be back, she thought with satisfaction. I wonder what size suit he wears? I think I'll buy him a nice wool one. I want my husband to look presentable.

Smiling, she went to the phone. She called her bank and ordered her account transferred to the all-night branch in Los Angeles. She wanted to have her money available so she could leave town to go to him the moment she found out where he lived: or (assuming he came to her) to have it handy so she could leave town with him the moment he proposed to her — even if it were in the middle of the night.

After that, she went to the door and put her hand through it.

I'm going to have to figure this out, she thought. If I figure out how I did it, I'm sure I can teach other people. I'm no different than they are; and I don't intend to be.

She went back to the bed and sat down and began to think. And she discovered that she could remember the greater part of everything she'd ever read.

IV

Calvin practiced teleportation for endless hours. He kept the metal ball Forential had given him in almost constant motion.

He would exclaim delightedly and hurl it toward one of the twenty-seven other mutants in his compartment. Until the time he hit John in the back of the head with it, his intended victims had always parried it. John lay in a pool of blood, and Calvin began to cry — loud, shrill wails of despair and contrition. When

Forential came, he knew instinctively what had happened.

Calvin represented the only failure the aliens had experienced in their mutation program; ten years ago his mind had ceased to develop. But for Forential's intercession, the council would have had him destroyed long ago; Forential, like a proud parent, kept hoping to overcome Calvin's heredity.

Forential waved his tentacles in exasperation. "You, here, Walt," he said. "We'll have to hurry. I'll show you how, and you can do it."

Walt, the most adept mutant in the compartment, listened attentively and then began to heal John. His face wrinkled in deep concentration. Flesh came together; blood ceased to flow; bone knitted. Forential grunted approval.

"Watch Walt, now," the alien instructed. "He's doing it nicely."

The others, breath held, watched.

At length John's head was healed. John stirred. He opened his eyes and looked about angrily. He stood up and hit Calvin in the face with his fist. Calvin, tears streaming down his cheeks, fingered his nose and sobbed brokenly. He put out a hand to touch Walt reassuringly.

Walt was his friend.

Walt — he had no other name — was six feet two inches tall, and, as Julia observed, handsome. His parents — he did not know this — were Americans; he had never seen them. He had been stolen from the hospital by Forential shortly after he was born. The alien, invisible, had come for him, clucked softly, wrapped him in a warm, invisible mantle, and taken him away; and the council of aliens had drawn a line through the names of another set of parents who had been exposed to the powerful, mutation-inducing field. Walt thought of Forential — in charge of their compartment — as a friend, as a parent, as a playmate, and as a counselor.

Shortly after Walt had healed John, the mutants of the smaller compartment gathered at the observation screen in the floor — or what was to them the floor: it was actually the broad rim of the wheel. They could look down at the screen and see a somewhat flickering image of Earth lying below their feet.

"Forential told us we'd get many strange powers . . ." one said.

Just before we went down to the planet, another completed the thought.

It's growing time, then.

They laughed together with excitement, and Calvin cracked his knuckles nervously.

"Let's play a trick on Forential," Calvin said. "Let's see if we can go through the bulkhead." His face was bright and hopeful. "Let's huh?"

Calvin raced to the far end of the compartment. "Come on!"

Like guilty children, they looked at one another. Then a few of them joined Calvin. *All right, let's.*

"Don't," Walt cautioned. "It's just machinery on the other side."

Why can't our thoughts penetrate it, then?

We aren't developed enough, Walt thought.

"Huh?" Calvin asked. He began pounding the bulk3head with his fist.

"No," one of the other mutants said. "Like this." He concentrated and tried to put a hand through the bulkhead.

We aren't developed enough.

Still the mutants continued. Since the aliens had stepped up the power in the two transmitters (power that closed the final connection in the mutants' brains and held it closed) the mutants were able to assault any problem with the full potentialities of the human brain. But even that was not enough. The aliens had planned carefully in order to keep the two mutant groups from discovering each other.

Forential came to make a special announcement. He spoke English with an accent that the mutants (who had learned the language from him) could not even imitate. As he surveyed them, his eyes shone with pride: they were a good, sturdy, healthy lot. "Children," he said. "Earth is now in the middle of a war. There will be little work left for us within another two months."

Calvin cried and waved his arms wildly and bounced the ball viciously around the room. Every earthman who killed an earthman was depriving him personally, of a victim. He wrung his hands.

"There'll be a thousand or so left, Calvin," Forential promised. "You must practice very diligently to be able to cope with them."

Calvin sniffed and shook his head. "I can kill that many in a minute. You stop the war, Forential, *please*."

"Think of it this way," Forential said. "The less work there is to do, the sooner you can return to your own planet."

"There's no earthmen to kill on Lyria," Calvin insisted stubbornly. "*Please* stop the war."

"I'll see what I can do." The alien smiled kindly. "You have the proper spirit. You are all very good children. You hurry, now, and practice all you can."

I can see Lyria's star now, Walt thought. We'll be home in another year, then. How welcome that will be. . . .

He had not broadcast the thought.

And suddenly, as if on another channel, another frequency, he felt Calvin in his mind and his mind in Calvin's — an odd, unexpected blending of thoughts that seemingly had occurred unconsciously.

Forential describes it so it is so pretty, our planet, Calvin was thinking: Green wartle rivers whack throw the ball at him, easy now . . . God, I hate those earthmen.

"I'll practice," Walt made Calvin say. He made Calvin hold the ball stationary. Then the contact between their minds was broken.

"Who did that?" Calvin demanded. "I'll hit him and break all his bones!"

Forential smiled sadly at Calvin and withdrew.

"It's nearly time," a mutant rejoiced. "God, I hate them, every one of them."

The mutants instinctively began forming their minds for the death radiation.

"They'll issue the rods shortly," Walt said.

Hatred blazed on Calvin's face. He had already forgotten about the contact a moment before. "I will kill them even without a rod."

"The radiation isn't lethal unless we have something to focus it with, remember that."

"With my hands!" Calvin cried happily. "I will kill them with my hands!"

Sweat beaded John's face. "There will be enough of killing."

It will be great pleasure to hunt them down.

They will kill some of us, Walt thought back. And, to himself: I wish I could be afraid.

Not me! Calvin thought joyously. It was uncertain when Calvin could telepath. *Not me!*

They have powerful weapons, too. Atom bombs, they are called. It will not be easy to kill them all. This thought came as a reminder from one of the aliens.

Calvin moved his powerful hands. "I can kill them all by myself."

The smaller compartment, itself, was huge. To the left lay the hydroponics tanks, and to the right, the mutants' cubicles. In the center of the compartment was the games space where the mutants boxed and wrestled and exercised with weights. The walls of each cubicle were so designed as to produce the illusion of great distances. The mutants would be required to face vast open spaces, and their cubicles partially conditioned them for the experience. Huge as their world was, it was miniscular compared to the one that would confront them.

Calvin, sitting beside Walt in Walt's cubicle, was trying to express an abstract concept.

". . . Forential is afraid of earthmen," he said. He puckered his face in a frown. "I have just thought of that."

"Forential is afraid of everything," Walt said respectfully.

"I remember once when I shoved him he was very afraid. I should*n't have," Calvin said. ". . . it must be wonderful to be afraid."

"He is more advanced than we are."

"We can kill earthmen, though," Calvin said. "He's too afraid to; so we get to kill them for him."

"You got it wrong; you always get things wrong. We are killing earthmen for ourselves."

"Oh, yes," Calvin nodded. "I forget"

"Forential is a friend," Walt said. "He helps the Lyrians from the goodness of his heart."

"Earthmen are very bad."

"That's right."

"They are a great evil," Calvin said excitedly.

"They must be killed."

"Yes, yes, yes!" Calvin agreed. "I will kill them with my hands." He fell silent, thinking.

". . . there is a Lyrian on Earth," Walt said slowly "I have been hearing her thoughts."

"I can think to you," Calvin said proudly. "Listen." He concentrated. Muscles in his jaws quivered. ". . . not today," he said sadly. "My brain . . . sometimes . . . you know? . . . sometimes. . . . "

"I am hearing thoughts from a Lyrian on Earth," Walt said in dull amazement. "Do you understand?"

"No; no."

"It's a female."

"All the females are on Lyria. . . . This is a man's work. We are . . . are going to fight for females, isn't that right?"

"I tell you," Walt said, "she's down there. The first time, I thought I was mistaken."

Calvin shook his head and flipped the ball toward an unseen mutant. "I can do that good," he said. The ball whistled back at him through the cubicle wall — leaving the wall unmarked as the atoms of one passed through the atomic spaces of the other. Happily, Calvin stopped it in mid flight.

"She's down there," Walt said. "I'll have to tell Forential about her."

Calvin tapped his head and smiled. "I think funny thoughts some times, too. You go see Forential. He can't help, but you go see him, Walt."

"I wasn't sure until just before you came in," Walt said.

"You go see him," Calvin said.

Walt stood up. "I was thinking with her just a little while ago. I don't understand it."

"I can think to you . . . some times."

"I'll be back," Walt said.

At the steel ladder leading up toward the alien section, Walt stopped and pressed the emergency-audience button. He waited for permission to ascend the ladder. Under no circumstance would he have ascended without it. The permissive light blinked.

He began to climb. At the ceiling hatch, he grunted and pressed against it with his shoulders. The hatch lifted away. He continued upward. Gravity lessened. His feet made soft, rustling noises.

He paused to rest at the first landing. He was in familiar territory. Fierut let the mutants from the smaller compartment help clean the machinery there every month or so. The air smelled of crisp ozone and hot oil.

Then as he rested, he saw movement behind one of the huge, softly purring machines. Although he could not know this, it was a female from the larger compartment. Muscles knotting, he waited.

He saw her again — the merest glint of flesh. She had not seen him. He half crouched.

It is impossible, he told himself. Only my compartment-mates and Forential and others of his race are on the ship.

Walt did not even think of trying for telepathic contact. Blind hatred overcame him. *She's an earthling!* he thought instinctively.

She has been left here for a test; that's it, he thought. Forential is testing me. . . .

He crept cautiously toward her. Still she was unaware of him.

I will break her neck, so. . . .

No, he thought suddenly.

Forential has brought her here for questioning. He would be angry if I harmed her. He does not intend it for a test after all.

He crouched undecided, trying to think. I better leave her, he thought.

He was motionless, watching. If I killed her, he thought, Forential might be angry.

He slipped silently toward the ladder.

Perhaps, he thought, Forential will give her to me to dispose of when he finishes with her.

He remembered seeing Forential dispose of several captured

earthlings. It was a very satisfying thing to watch. Forential promised us some, Walt thought, but he never gave us any. But I guess I was wrong in thinking he was too cowardly to risk another trip to Earth for them. . . .

Just as he reached the ladder, he whirled. The female had seen him. She had started toward him. His eyes sparkled in anticipation.

She's a Lyrian! he thought in amazement.

Damned earthmen, she thought.

No, I. . . .

For a long moment they were motionless. Then Walt, keeping a suspicious eye on her until he was above the second ceiling continued to climb.

In the alien compartment, the gravity was so low that Walt almost floated. He propelled himself toward Forential's cubicle.

"Come in," Forential said, sensing him. Forential looked up when he entered.

"I saw a female Lyrian in the machinery room!" Walt blurted.

There was a moment of silence. Forential's face grew a shade paler. ". . . did she see you?"

Of course, Walt thought.

It was an effort for Forential to telepath in English. He preferred vocalizing. Staring at Walt with his faceted, unblinking eyes, he thought in his own language, a language earthlings were incapable of learning: ★★Lycan, you idiot! You told me the machinery room was clear! One of my charges has seen one of yours!★★

★★I have great regret,★★ Lycan answered. ★★I — I overlooked her.★★

★★We cannot risk the compartments discovering each other.★★ Forential thought angrily.

"This is not all," Walt said. *There is one on Earth!*

Forential's tentacles stiffened. What? It was almost involuntary: unbelieving: terrified.

"There *is* one on Earth. A female."

★★I have regretfully disposed of the one he saw,★★ Lycan telepathed. ★★Have you disposed of the one who saw her?★★

★★*Send out a call for the Council!*★★ Forential broadcast hysterically. ★★One more set of parents than we were aware of was exposed to our field! *There is an unindoctrinated mutant on Earth!*★★

"Are you sure?" Forential demanded of Walt.

"What about the one I saw a minute ago?" Walt persisted.

". . . she came on the last ship from Lyria," Forential lied curtly.

"Oh? I would like to talk to her. We all would. Can we, Forential?"

The alien was outwardly impassive. "We'll see. Never mind her right now. Tell me about this one on Earth."

"I heard her thoughts."

Forential lay his tentacles on his desk. They scrabbled nervously. "How long have you known?" How did she manage to break through our telepathic shielding? he wondered. He made an inward snarl of surprise . . . powerful mind! . . . Then he went weak with temporary relief: Suppose we hadn't found out about her until the invasion? We had to know now while there's time! How much does she . . . ?

"Just today, for sure. Once or twice before. . . ."

Walt told Forential all he knew about Julia. He spoke quickly, and with rising excitement.

BY the time he was finished, the council had convened. The circuits were open. Forential fed them the information Walt had just given him. Their incomprehensible language crackled beyond Walt's thought range.

★★We must destroy her at once.★★

★★Unconditioned! Unconditioned: no telling how much information she has.★★

A terrified thought: ★★Danger, danger, danger!★★

Forential's eyes did not leave Walt's face. His thoughts were assessing the situation even under the force of the shock. . . . The one called Julia had to be under the influence of the larger transmitter; all the mutants had been bred for that frequency. It was only years later that the ones in the smaller com★partment had been adjusted to the other frequency. If the larger, transmitter were to be shut down, then it would interrupt Lycan's training schedule for nearly a thousand mutants. But it would also render Julia an earth-normal. . . .

". . . we'll try to teleport her here," Forential said. "You have had contact with her. Can you regain it?"

"I think, yes."

"I will explain the process," Forential said.

"Yes . . . yes . . . ," Walt said from time to time as he listened. He nodded his head excitedly. "I have it! I understand! I can do it!"

"You are in contact with her through the shielding? Do not think of her now. Just touch her. Can you?"

"Yes," Walt said.

"You feel the grip on her I explained?" Forential said eagerly.

"Yes!"

Now yank her!

Walt yanked.

Julia didn't budge.

". . . I slipped," Walt said apologetically. Sweat glistened on his upper lip.

"Try again!" Forential ordered.

★★Cut the power in the big transmitter,★★ he instructed.

The aliens had been unwilling to complete their mutations. To do so would have given the mutants too much autonomy. By arranging to have the final effects dependent upon the transmission of certain frequency impulses, the aliens could — in the unlikely event of difficulty with their charges — reduce them to earth-normals by the flick of a switch. It also was an arrangement necessary to their invasion plan. The aliens were careful.

★★It's cut.★★

A moment later, Walt said, "She's changed!"

(The mutants in the larger compartment had ceased to be able to hear or put their hands through walls.)

Now! Forential ordered.

A pause.

Walt let out his breath in an explosive burst. He shook his head. "It's no use. I can't."

Forential's tentacles went limp. He had known it was impossible to teleport higher life forms against their resistance; he had hoped she would have been caught off guard.

★★Cut the transmitter in again,★★ Forential thought wearily.

★★*She'll have to be killed,*★★ Lycan projected with an undertone of terror.

★★Send him down,★★ Fierut, the engineer, suggested, trembling in fear. ★★Since he has potential knowledge of the other compartment, he will have to be destroyed anyway if he remains. Send him down to kill her.★★

★★We can cut off his transmitter when the main force strikes. He can't do us any harm down there ....★★

"You'll have to go down and kill her," Forential told Walt. "She is a clever, clever traitor...."

"Give me the focus rod, so I can practice the death radiation with it," Walt said eagerly.

Forential answered smoothly, with scarcely an instant's hesitation; but during that time, he explored the situation and his answer was a considered one. "No, you'll have to go unarmed. We can't run the risk of premature exposure."

★★Stress that,★★ the Elder insisted.

"I can kill earthmen, too?"

"Just her," Forential said, knowing Walt would obey him. "Just her," he repeated for emphasis. "Remember that. Approach her carefully. Do not let her suspect what you intend to do. Lie to her, Walt, anything to get close to her, and then...."

★★I'll get a ship ready for him,★★ Lycan thought. ★★And some suitable clothes.★★

"May I tell my mates goodbye?" Walt asked.

★★Don't forget he has seen the one from the other compartment,★★ the Elder reminded Forential sharply.

"No," Forential lied. "You haven't the time. You must leave immediately."

★★Tell him much depends on him,★★ the Elder thought.

"I can't overstress the importance of this," Forential said. He too, was trembling now as he began to see the possible implications; his tentacles quivered. His faceted eyes peered deeply into Walt's face.

"It will be a great service to Lyria and to all the people of your race."

★★It is a good planet,★★ Lycan thought. ★★We can't lose it

now!★★

★★We've already begun to breed for the gravity,★★ one of the others thought plaintively.

★★By rights it should be ours.★★

★★The air is so good, so rich. . . . ★★

★★We can't lose it now!★★ Lycan insisted pathetically.

★★Savages: the thought of the natives horrifies me! *Hurry Forential!*★★

Forential thought to them with all the conviction he could muster: ★★This child of mine is very adept. He will kill her.★★

"The ship will have to be destroyed as soon as you land," Forential told the mutant. "That means you will have to remain until the invasion. Let me review all this again. . . . "

Walt's hands jerked with nervous anticipation. "I understand, Forential."

★★The ship is ready any time, Forential.★★

"Let me review this again. . . . "

As Walt listened, he thought; I wonder if earthmen can prevent themselves from being teleported? I hope not. I want to teleport them this way and that way, from all around me, whenever one comes close to me. It's the easiest way to kill them. It's a shame I couldn't get the one on Earth. . . . She would have suddenly materialized, bloody, twisted, wrenched, turned inside out ★ — a beautiful corpse; that's what we should do with earthlings, and with traitors.

★★Lycan: Hurry with your charges.★★

★★One more week, Elder. And they will be ready to attack!★★

V

The thing Walt first noticed was the hugeness of space around his tiny, falling ship. Through the viewplate above him — he was supine — the vast, star-set blackness seemed infinite, seemed to suck his mind out of his body until it was connected only by a tenuous thread. He had seen space from the great wheel that was dwindling behind him; but never before had its immediacy been impressed on him with such force: here, it was an intimate wrapping, clutching at him from all sides.

He had pointed out as nearly as he could determine it from brief, telepathic contact (the aliens showed him how to center on her) Julia's location on the planet. The aliens had promised to land him in an unpopulated area on the same part of the continent. The aliens' thoughts did not come through the shielding around their space station; nor did the thoughts of his compartment-mates. For the first time in his life, he was terribly alone.

Earth grew in the viewplate; expanding majestically to obliterate the surrounding space, it grew shimmery along its almost regular circumference. The orbit of his saucer-shaped ship flattened into a great spiral. The ship twisted around the Earth from shadow to light and then into shadow again as if it were attached to the loose end of a piece of string being wound up by the slowly turning planet. Gravity pressed his body, crushed him; a sudden, sickening drop left him weightless.

The aliens maneuvered his ship carefully. Walt could not — as the aliens could — be immersed in a liquid tank to make possible instantaneous changes of direction. They let him down tenderly.

Hello, Julia thought brightly.

It was frightening. Here was a Lyrian whose mind had pierced even the wheel's shielding! How could he hope to kill her?

He stared at the approaching planet, and his hands tightened beneath the pressing layers of the acceleration cocoon that enfolded him.

But I, he thought: I was able to contact her through the shielding, too. I was the only one who did; nobody else reported her. It's all right: she's no stronger than I am.

I know you're there, she thought.

I'll wait to answer, he thought; he tried to hold his mind shut.

You're traveling very fast: Much too fast!

The ship lurched a bit, slowing down. Then — for several seconds — he was as much in Calvin's mind as his own; their minds blended. The shielding did not stop that. Calvin was waiting at the foot of the ladder for him to return. *Don't wait,* Walt thought; *I'm —* And as unexpectedly as it had commenced, the blending ceased; he was once again alone. *Calvin! Calvin!* he thought.

No answer. Calvin's abnormal, unpredictable mind remained inaccessible.

Hello, Julia said sweetly. The complacency she conveyed, the assurity of her thought, the self confidence, the self reliance — these things troubled him.

The ship touched ground, bounced once and was still. The switch above him flipped over with a nasty, metallic snicker. In a fever of haste, he ripped out of the cocoon. He had less than twenty seconds to get outside before the molecular reaction set in.

His feet pounded to the door; his hand found the lever; his body fell hard against the surface. The door popped open and he sprawled across the cool sand.

He was up and running.

At fifty yards he looked back panting. The ship began to glow a dull, unexciting dun color. A wave of heat pressed against his cheek. The ship folded upon itself and collapsed into a powder of dry, red rust.

The desert around him was endless; the chill of distance from which he was completely unprotected caught in his throat. He sat down and huddled up to protect himself from it. He trembled violently and whimpered for Forential. Cold sweat drenched his body . . .

He forced himself to stand; slowly the reaction passed. He opened his eyes. He took a deep, nervous breath and let it out.

And —

He wanted to fall to the ground and dig his fingers into it.

Good God! he thought. She's trying to teleport me to her! She had caught him unaware, when the terror of the desert was still upon him. He could not marshal his thoughts to resist her.

He twisted frantically. *Watch out! You'll kill me!*

The attempt ceased at once.

. . . oh? I thought . . . Yes, I can see now that . . . The thought ended abruptly. There was an utter and terrifying silence from her direction.

His mind began to add up the overall situation with great speed. Hello. She did not answer. He licked his lips.

I wasn't, he thought, *... I wasn't serious when I tried to teleport you a while ago. I was just playing a joke on you. I wasn't trying to kill you.*

She seemed to be thinking the statement over. *If you had tried again, I would have let you. I didn't realize it was you at first.*

He cursed himself.

You were moving too fast a moment ago.

He was getting her position fixed. She lay west. He turned in that direction. She broke the contact.

Search planes of the Air Force began to drone over the area; searching for the saucer the radar had tracked to earth.

Walt walked for hours across the desert. His feet, unaccustomed to the tight fitting shoes, pained him. He grew weary. Occasionally, lights from the highway to his left winked by in the night. On he trudged. Sand crept into his shoes.

Dawn came. He looked toward the mountains, blue with distance. He would not be able to make them. Soon the sun would be overhead. The heat (it was already promised) would be intense. He would have to have water. I could change the sand to water — the air — the plants, he thought. (Forential could, he told himself.) I could: If I only knew more; if I only had practice. If I could only see just how water is put together. Forential should have explained things like that to us.

Hello, he thought to Julia.

He received no answer.

She's suspicious, he thought. What did I do to make her suspicious? She wasn't when I first contacted her. But there was something funny about her. . . . Maybe she knows I know she's a traitor. Forential said lie to her.

Hello, he thought. *I'm a Lyrian traitor, too.*

Julia, he thought. *Where are you?*

Damn her: she isn't going to answer.

He looked at the mountains. He was walking automatically now.

Forential has confidence in me, he thought. Or else he'd have given me more instructions. He knows I can get there. It's up to me to do it, that's all. . . . Well, I can't make the mountains by walking. . . .

He crossed to the highway; he dreaded his first contact with earthlings.

It was a broad, gleaming band of concrete, six lanes wide with foot high rails between lanes, broken, each mile, by changeover slots.

Early morning sun cut down from the east.

Cars came by like bullets. Whirrr, whish, and they were gone.

He waved at the ones going west, but they were past him almost before he saw them. The trucks on the inner lanes were ladened streaks; the car traffic on the middle one was varicolored blurs. A streamlined bus flashed silver and dwindled to a spot in the distance.

. . . Moving more slowly, a passenger car came down the outer lane.

Walt waved desperately. Thirst was already on him.

The car squealed to a stop. He ran toward it.

It was his first view of an earthman. His stomach knotted with revulsion; his body shook with hatred. All his life he had been conditioned to kill them on sight.

"Where's your car?" the driver asked when he came abreast.

Walt gestured vaguely. His face contorted with the effort he made to control his hands.

"Why'n hell didn't ya radio in for a pick-up? God, man, you could die out here."

Walt said: "You let me go with you?"

"Sure . . . get in."

Walt fumbled at the side of the car.

"Push the button, you dope."

Walt pushed the button, and the door opened.

"Aintcha never seen a car before?"

Walt grunted and got in.

"You been here long?"

If he doesn't shut up, I'll strangle him, Walt thought. He closed the door and pressed against it to be as far away from the earthling as possible.

"Somebody probably saw you when they passed and radioed on you," the driver said, starting the car and flipping it on automatic. "A pick-up'll be along shortly. This will save you the fee."

Walt gritted his teeth. "Thanks."

". . . you gotta funny accent. Where you from?"

"I don't want to talk to you," Walt said slowly. God, he thought, I wish Forential hadn't told me not to kill any of them!

The driver looked sideways at him, shrugged, and began to whistle through his teeth.

Ah, to kill him, Walt thought. To kill him! He stared at the man's heavy jowls. To rip into them. . . . Wait, wait until Julia is caught, just wait. . . . I want to kill her a little at a time.

Beyond the blue mountains, the driver drew the car into the checker stand.

"Got any fruit?" the California state inspector asked.

The driver climbed out and called the officer aside. They whispered. Walt twisted uncomfortably. His spine began to prickle.

The officer came over and opened Walt's door. "Get out, buddy."

"Me?"

"You. Hurry up!"

Walt's eyes darted rapidly about. He got out slowly.

"Say something!"

"I, I don't know. What do you want me to say something for?"

"It's Russian?" the driver demanded.

"Hell, I don't know. Come on buddy." The officer took Walt's arm. "There's something funny here all right."

Russian? Walt thought. What did that mean? He could tell he was in for trouble. The man's grip on his arm was uncomfortably authoritative. If I only had a focus rod, I could . . . , he thought.

His heart began to hammer. Would they use one of the terrible atom bombs to destroy him in another minute?

"Come along," the officer said.

"...I want a drink of water, please."

"He's been out on the desert," the driver said. "Maybe all night, from the looks of him."

"Okay," the officer said. "Let's go over here ... What's your name?"

Walt walked beside him. "Walt."

"Walt what?"

"...Walt."

"I mean, Walt Smith or Jones or Johnson?"

"That's it." Walt's mind raced.

"What?"

"Johnson," Walt said. "Walt Johnson?"

The officer puckered up his lips. "Okay, friend, we'll find out more about you in a little bit. Let's get your drink."

They entered the warm roadside office. The officer crossed to the cooler and drew a glass of water.

"Thanks." Walt drank thirstily. "More?"

The officer complied; as yet he had not taken his eyes off the mutant.

Holding his glass, empty for a second time, Walt glanced around the office, balancing nervously on the balls of his feet. When his eyes rested on a spot behind the officer, he said, "What's that?"

The officer turned. "What?"

Walt tried to concentrate on the invisibility projection. He started for the door.

"What?" the officer repeated, puzzled. He looked around. "I'll be damned! Now where —"

Once in the yard, Walt raced toward the check point. It was hard to hold the distortion field around himself and his clothing.

The officer was now in the yard shouting.

"He can't get far!" someone called.

A moment later a car drew up to the check point. Walt would have to pass through the steel of the door to enter it unnoticed. Steel was difficult to penetrate, particularly difficult, if he remained invisible while doing it.

He succeeded.

He settled into the rear seat.

Blood vessels strained on his forehead.

Hurry! he thought.

THE driver meshed the gears with a button just when he was wavering on the edge of visibility. An officer glanced into the car. Walt held his breath. The officer motioned the car on.

The driver, Walt saw now, was a girl. Forential had shown him pictures of female Lyrians; and this girl — but for the fact she was an earthling — would have been beautiful. Now that he had begun to master his hate reaction, he felt the stirrings of curiosity.

He became visible.

After a mile or so, she must have heard his breathing. The car was on automatic, following the guide beam on the center of the lane. She turned. She studied him for a long moment with beautiful grey eyes.

"Hello, where did you come from?"

Walt moved his lips.

The girl was sizing him up carefully. She seemed to like what she saw. She nodded. "You got on back there? I didn't see you."

Walt stared at her.

"You wanted a lift, that's it, isn't it?"

Walt said nothing. She wore soft perfume. If I did not hate her so much . . . he thought.

"You deaf and dumb."

". . . no. No."

She pulled the car into a clear-lane niche.

She regarded him. "Not bad. . . . Get up front."

He obeyed her. She started the car again.

"I'm Walt Johnson."

"Where are you going, Walt Johnson?"

"This . . . down this way." The emotions were almost out of control with excitement. His thoughts were becoming powerful and diffuse.

You let her alone! Julia ordered.

It was like a slap. He quickly dampened his thoughts. Hatred returned.

The driver of the car chewed gum reflectively, watching him. She twitched nervously closer.

She saw his eyes. She stopped chewing gum. Perhaps she saw the hatred. She was trembling, suddenly. "You. . . ." She drew the car into a niche again. "You better get out here."

Walt was angry. No killing, no killing, he told himself. He controlled his hands. He forced himself to open the door and get out.

"Somebody'll give you a ride," the girl said.

The car moved away, gaining speed quickly. . . .

An orchard lay behind him. Cars passed more slowly now that the desert was to the east.

Walt began to walk.

He thought: Forential told us a while ago there was a destructive war in progress. It doesn't seem like there's a war. I haven't seen any signs of it. It's peaceful. I wonder what he meant?

Within a few minutes, a car drew along side of him.

"I'm Walt Johnson. I'm going down the road."

"Get in, then."

Walt got in.

Hello, Julia, he thought. *I want to see you, Julia.*

VI

In the space station, Forential sat in his cubicle in mental conference with the other aliens. Behind their flow of thoughts was the unreferred-to but ever-present fear for their own lives. Cowardice was taken for granted; it was so deeply a part of their own culture (if it wasn't somehow a racial characteristic) that it did not need to be acknowledged.

The aliens always let other races fight their wars of conquest.

Forential knew that his own personal existence might well hinge on the outcome of the next few hours. None of the aliens knew how much knowledge Julia possessed. Unlike the other mutants, she had not been kept in ignorance of the basic laws of nature. How dangerous she might be, they could only guess. Was she capable of attacking them?

Forential was physically ill; he wanted to flee. If he had had a ship capable of traveling interstellar distances, he would have embarked without delay. But the huge interstellar ship of his race would not be back for another thirty years. There was no escape from the space station; there was no place to go.

And if the earthlings were not destroyed, if the invasion of Earth failed, retaliation from the planet would not be long coming. Once the Earth located the space station (and Earth would, once Earth realized its existence) even human normals would be able to destroy it — one rocket with an atomic war head would do — long before the interstellar ship returned.

Walt could not fail; the invasion could not fail.

★★Let's try to make peace with the earthings,★★ one of the aliens thought. ★★It's better than . . . than exposing *ourselves* to physical violence!★★

★★That would be suicide: once they realized what we had been planning to do to them.★★

★★I don't trust them.★★

★★Let Forential send down all his charges to kill the female!★★

★★Don't be hysterical!★★ the Elder thought hysterically.

Forential knew that to send down his charges first might alert Earth to the danger of invasion: twenty-seven saucer-ships would not go unnoticed. But even if they would, even if Earth remained unaware, such a course would completely disrupt the plan of conquest.

★★She hasn't realized the menace yet,★★ the Elder thought. ★★Walt will kill her. Walt will kill her, won't he, Forential?★★

★★Yes.★★ If only one of us went to make sure, Forential thought. To help him . . . no . . . None of us would risk it. It's too dangerous.

The aliens did not have any equipment to make their single person ships invisible. It took bulky distortion machinery; the single person ships were too large to cover with mental shielding.

Twenty years ago, yes (Forential thought) we could have risked it. But now the radar screens around all the major countries are too tight. We could not, like Walt, destroy our ship. We would need it to return in.

We must give him all the help we can, Forential thought.

We must.

We must.

Lycan, the Elder thought. **Can you cut the power of your charges?**

An extended period might have a bad psychological effect . . .

They won't realize the implication — that they're not Lyrians, that we control them — until too late.

If we could give Walt twelve hours, Forential thought. ** . . . we've got to give him every chance!**

When do you think he'll be close to her? the Elder asked.

Forential consulted his maps. He calculated rapidly.

If he travels fast — if he has luck — by another five hours.

Lycan, the Elder instructed, **continue with training until then. We'll cut off the greater transmitter five hours from now. Twelve hours should give Walt more than enough time to kill her. It will be mutant trying to kill an earth-normal. He can't fail!**

He can't fail, they echoed nervously.

Will twelve hours be enough?

If he does, somehow, fail, we can't risk delaying the invasion more than that.

I will see that it doesn't delay the invasion, Lycan promised. **I'll train them right through normalcy.**

Walt had arrived in Hollywood.

Wait for me there, Julia (dressing carefully) projected to him. *I'll be right over to get you.*

She finished combing her hair. She went to her handbag, snapped it closed decisively, and slipped it over her arm. She was smiling.

On her way out of the room, she picked up the book on brain surgery that she hadn't yet had the chance to read. She skimmed through it in the taxi on the way to pick Walt up.

She paused a fraction of a second over one of the illustrations; in that time, she was able to memorize it. My brain, she thought, is different right there; but I can't see my own brain well enough to tell much; I want to look at his for a minute if I can.

Having finished the book, she held it primly in her lap, tapping impatiently on it with her fingers.

There's a lot of things funny about this boy, she thought. I've got to get more information about him. I've got a suspicion he's going to be in for a few surprises.

(It was less than an hour before the aliens would cut off the larger transmitter.)

When I first located him for sure, she thought, he was traveling *much* too fast; faster and higher than any experimental rocket I've ever heard of.

I've got to check on the old flying saucer reports, she thought. They're the only things I can remember reading about that were supposed to move that fast.

"This is him waiting up here," Julia said to the driver. "Just pull over to the curb."

A moment later, opening the door, she said, "Get in. I'm Julia."

"I'm Walt Johnson," he said, flexing his hands. "Let's go someplace where we can be alone."

"Well," she said. "It's good to see you, Walt." She extended her hand.

He had sealed off his thoughts. His hand was moist in hers; it responded uncertainly to her warm pressure. She drew him inside. She caught a wisp of thought that he was not quite able to conceal. "Back to the hotel," she told the driver.

Now I'm *sure*, she thought, that he really tried to teleport me out of my hotel room. I wonder why he wanted to? Why should he want to kill me?

I'll have to keep an eye on him. But he's such a baby. He can't even control his emotions.

"Your clothing," she said, studying him with professional concern, "is all wrong. We'll just have to get some more. Some to fit your personality better. I'll do that tomorrow."

Anger crossed his face. He rubbed his hand over his knee and looked down at his trousers. "I like them," he said in a surly voice.

She was not afraid of him. She had no need to be. He was such an innocent!

Why, she thought, he doesn't seem to have any information to draw on hardly at all; he'll be harmless as long as I wish him so.

"I'm a Lyrian traitor, too," he said.

"You are?"

His accent. She could not remember any accent on Earth like that. He had not learned his English from an earthman. A Lyrian had taught him?

"What are you doing here?" he said.

Boy! she thought. Is his conversation naive! Keep him talking, girl!

She studied his face. She thought: Get 'em young and raise 'em to suit yourself, Julia.

SHE added up the facts she had already discovered. He was, like herself, a human mutant. (I must check, she thought, to see if there were any human babies missing during the last flying saucer scare twenty-four years ago, the year I was born.) The mutants had been collected at birth, but the collectors had overlooked her. Walt had traveled here from (where? Mars? Luna?) in order to rectify this oversight by putting her out of the way. Why? Obviously he owed allegiance to the collectors (Lyrians?) from whom he had probably learned — among other things — his atrocious accent. He was —

She had ignored his question, so he asked another one. "Where is the war?"

"War? Julia repeated. She frowned delicately. "There's no war. Not right now. The international situation is getting better, I think." War? she asked herself. He's got a lot of misinformation about us.

She kept trying to *see* into the physical structure of his brain. Ah, she thought, yes. Right there —

A bridge there, all right.

It's probably an easy mutation, she thought. Probably latent in everyone's genes. The next development of man? (But how many centuries will it take for it to come out again?) How did the collectors produce the mutation in the first place — assuming they did produce (as well as harvest) it?

Could, she thought, a surgeon — operate, as it were — on an adult brain to produce the bridge? . . . I'll have to take up surgery. A few months to learn technique. I think I could. It's easy to heal, because of the subconscious pattern (the cellular pattern?) but to — operate — to change — to build into a different structure, so that would require experiments and study, perhaps actual knife work. . . .

"There *has* to be a war," Walt said. "Forential told us there was."

"There isn't. Not now." Forential? A non-human? An alien?

"He told us," Walt said.

"He lied," Julia said.

"He doesn't lie."

Julia shrugged. Walt is a loyal follower, she thought. "There's no war. Maybe he meant there would be one shortly; maybe it was a premature announcement." Lord! do these aliens have some way of prodding the Russian bear? she thought. Or how the devil are they — Forentials, wherever they are — thinking of starting a war?

Walt refused to consider her denial. He did not look her in the face. "I like you," he said. He was desperate to change the subject. "Your smile. You're so . . . so . . ." *nice.* He thought the last word; he took the risk that she might peep his other thoughts. He was almost certain she could not; he hoped to peep hers if she thought a reply. Forential couldn't be a liar!

Julia knew they were both incorrect: his statement and his conviction. But she liked to hear him say he liked her. I guess, she thought, he's trying to lull my suspicions. Maybe I better lull his, too. . . .

She smiled sweetly.

"You see, I've never seen a Lyrian female before," Walt said. ". . . except one on the ship just the other day; but just one, before."

Is Lyria supposed to be a *planet*? she thought to herself. "You've never been to Lyria, then, have you?"

". . . we were very young when we left."

He doesn't even know he's a native of Earth! Julia thought. "You know," she said, "I'll bet I know more about you than you think I do."

That brought a fear reaction from Walt.

You don't need to be afraid of me, Julia thought soothingly.

(She had scarcely half an hour left before the aliens shut off the big transmitter.)

"How soon. . . . When will we get to the hotel?"

"Soon, now," Julia said.

"We'll be alone?" Walt said.

"We'll have a chance to talk; there are a lot of things for us to talk about."

"Yes," he said. He began to rub his hands over one another. His growing excitement and his hatred bubbled just below the surface of his mind; Julia could feel the emotions without him being aware that she could.

My, she thought. He's going to take a lot of re-educating before he makes a very good husband.

When they entered the hotel room, Walt found his throat expanding with excitement.

Forential, he thought, will be pleased that I have killed her in secret. No one on Earth will ever know who she was killed by. When she is dead, I can slip out of the hotel and . . . and invisible, I can steal food and drink and stay in empty rooms until the invasion comes; and when it does, then I can start teleporting earthlings and slaying them with my hands, and. . . . She doesn't suspect, he thought, that I am going to kill her in just a moment.

He complimented himself on how cleverly he had concealed his intentions.

Covertly he surveyed the room. The pitcher on the table? The chair? What with? A sudden numbing blow — like the blow Calvin delivered to John. Then, afterwards, hands, knees, fingers — and she will be dead.

He saw himself rising triumphant from her still body. Saw Forential (when, later, he heard of it) smiling approval, saw his mates listening awe struck. . . . His breath trembled in his throat; his arms ached to be moving.

"Won't you sit down?" she said.

I will wait until she is off guard, he thought. Smiling in anticipation, he sat down.

. . . she doesn't, he thought, seem like a traitor. Such bright, clear eyes. She seems, so nice, so trusting, so innocent. It was foolish to have been afraid of meeting her. She's small and harmless. I wish she weren't a traitor; maybe —

But Forential knows.

(How about the war? Why did Forential say there was a war?)

Forential knows. He said to kill her.

Julia, studying him with faint amusement, said "Have you looked at your brain? I have a picture of a human brain here. I want to show you how alike they are."

"Lyrians have a superficial resemblance to earthlings."

"Look at this. Very similar. The same, almost."

Walt shifted uneasily. Her eyes did not move from his face. What was she getting at?

"I wonder," she said, "why we . . . Lyrians . . . have had certain powers given to us just recently? Why, before, we were no different than earthlings?"

Walt frowned. He didn't want to think about it. He had a job to do.

"There's a — call it — a bridge in our minds. It's just recently been closed."

(It was ten minutes before the larger transmitter was to be turned off for twelve hours.)

Walt decided on the pitcher. The answer to her question was suddenly obvious. "That means we're ready to invade."

She watched him very closely. Her fingers tapped her knee. ". . . you said you were on a ship?"

It's almost time to kill her, he thought. I'm sorry, he wanted to say: but I really must. "Yes. A space station."

"How many of you are there?"

"Twenty-seven; twenty-eight, counting me."

"That's not many. Not enough." She bent forward. "You said

you saw a Lyrian female on the ship. I think there's another group of Lyrians on the ship. I think they're going to invade first. That's the war your group is supposed to come in on the end of. You're going to be used as a clean-up group."

"Forential would have told us," Walt said.

"The question is: *Why didn't he tell you?*"

Walt realized how terribly sly and dangerous she was. She was too smart to be harmless. Suppose she should warn — but who could she warn? Earthlings? Could they get their atom bombs ready?

He felt his skin prickle. *Look behind you!* he thought to her. It had worked with the officer; it worked with her.

She turned.

Savagely, he grasped the pitcher with the mental fingers of teleportation. He hurled it as hard as he could at the back of her head.

Julia was ready for the blow. She had the molecules of the pitcher displaced before it was half way to her. It passed through her body easily and smashed against the far wall.

She turned quickly enough to avoid Walt's rush.

On her feet now, she wavered into partial displacement.

Snarling harshly, he advanced on her.

(There was less than five minutes remaining. One of the aliens hovered at the larger transmitter.)

He tried to grab her. His hand passed through her body.

She smiled.

He tried to adjust to her level of displacement. He choked. Quickly he realized what was wrong; he rectified the air so he could breathe. She changed to normal just as he sprang. He hurtled through her as through the air itself.

She turned to face him. He was panting. "When I was a kid," she said, "I used to throw rocks when I got mad."

Damn you! His fists clenched. He towered over her.

She did not have any more time to waste with him. 'That means,' he had said, 'we're ready to invade.'

How much time did she have? The full extent of the menace was gradually taking form in her mind. With an army of indoctrinated mutants. . . . Invasion! Murder! Destruction! For an instant she wanted to collapse and cry like a frightened little girl.

What am I going to do? what am I going to do? what am I going to do? she thought frantically.

I've got to see someone! I've got to convince someone — I've got to show people my mutant powers: they'll have to believe me! The President, the Army. . . .

How much time?

She made a distortion field. Invisible, she rushed to the door. She paused, returned for her handbag. Holding it, she passed through the door.

I haven't got time to beat reason into his head, she thought. I'll tend to him later.

Half way down the stairs, she suddenly became visible.

VII

Oh, damn! she thought. This happened once before. How long will it last this time?

A great chill exploded in her body.

. . . suppose — ?

Now she ran in earnest. Her legs moved like pistons. The few patrons in the lobby glanced up in disapproval. At the door she almost bowled over a young man with a brown sack full of quarts of beer.

Once in the street, she stopped and darted frightened glances about her. It was growing dark. Neon winked. The street was unnatural and brittle under the artificial lights. Well dressed women, serious and unsmiling (serenely confident that they were being mistaken for movie stars) walked beside athletic escorts; sales girls and office clerks window shopped intently.

At the curb Julia almost danced with nervousness.

He can come upon me invisible! she thought. He can throw things! He can —! *I can't even tell when he's near me!*

She waved desperately for a cab.

"Cab! Cab! Taxi!"

It receded toward Vine Street.

Even now he's coming out of the hotel! she thought. Or he sees me from the Window! . . . I can't wait here; I'll have to run; I'll. . . .

A chartreuse convertible with its top up drew to a stop in front of her. The driver opened the door by pressing a button on the dash. The upholstery was made of tiger skin. He smiled nervously. "Going down this way?"

She hesitated only an instant. "My God, yes!" she said.

"Get in."

She got in and slammed the door. "Let's go! mister."

"When you're in a hurry, these cabs . . . you never can find one."

He wore a sports jacket, most of which was canary yellow. He had thin, delicate hands; his face was lean and sunless; his eyes were sad and misunderstood. The hands threaded the convertible into traffic.

Julia fidgeted. She kept glancing behind her.

"Somebody following you?"

Julia shuddered. "I hope not."

The driver waited. Julia did not amplify; she was half turned now, so she could see out the rear window.

"I had to talk to someone," the driver said apologetically. "I was driving along, and suddenly I had to talk to someone. You know how it is? . . . Then there you were; you seemed in such a hurry."

"I'm sure glad you stopped, mister!"

"I mean," the driver said intently, "I get wanting to *talk*. My name's Green. You may have heard of me. I produce pictures — motion pictures. I'm a producer."

How can I ever get away from Walt! Julia thought. He can run me down whenever he wants to!

"Nobody hears of producers," the driver said. "That's all right with me. Let other people take the credit. I don't like to call attention to myself." He brought out a monogrammed cigarette case and flicked it open. "Cigarette?"

"No, no, thank you." Julia twisted at the strap of her handbag.

"Who can you talk to, I mean really? All *they're* after is your money. . . . I'll tell you what I really want. I want a farm — no, don't laugh: it's the truth — a little piece of land. I want to settle down, you know. Most people don't understand how it is." He gazed sadly down Hollywood Boulevard. "To be famous, I mean."

Julia was scarcely listening. She bit her lip.

"My wife, now, she's an actress. In her next picture, she opens a beer can with her teeth. Not a bottle; anyone can open a bottle. She doesn't understand me. She's an actress." One of his delicate hands moved over the tiger skin toward Julia. "I'd like — sometimes to get away. Go away for a weekend. Some place where they'd never heard of A. P. Green, the big producer. You know. I wish — I honestly wish I weren't — some times."

The hand touched Julia's dress. She was too preoccupied to notice.

". . . you have an interesting face. It's very, very expressive. I want to give you my card. I want you to come in for a test."

Julia moved away from him. All she could think about was Walt. Could he be in that car just behind? ". . . please . . . ?" she said vaguely in protest.

He blinked his eyes; the hand retreated a few inches. "I've never talked to anyone like this before," he said. "But your face, your eyes. . . . When I saw you standing there — saw you were running from something — I knew you'd understand."

Julia swallowed stiffly. She pivoted to face him. "Listen mister. I need help. Would you drive me into L. A.? Fast, mister?"

He was hurt. He drew back. "I thought we could go. . . . I know a little place. . . . They know me there; we could eat, and —" He moved one hand pathetically.

Julia felt a flutter of thought. (There was still a tiny bit of residual power remaining; it was fading fast.) Walt was starting after her!

"Mister, for God's sake, *can you drive me into L. A.?* I've got to get some money out of the all-night bank!"

". . . yes, of course, yes." He moved his lips without words. "I thought you'd understand. Your face. . . . Nobody does, really. How it is, I mean."

"Please hurry," she said. If I can just get a car before Walt catches me, she thought. That's the only way I can keep away from him. I've got to keep moving until I get my powers back; or until . . . until . . . what? Her lower lip trembled. She was cold and numb. *Hurry!* she wanted to shriek.

For a full minute Walt did not realize she was gone. When he did, he was relieved. He found himself trembling. Where did that demon go? Thank God she's gone; I — !

The thought of her, diminutive and infinitely superior, made him cringe. He was afraid of her. He wanted to cry.

Forential understands, Walt thought. If he were here now, he'd understand. He'd . . . he'd tell me what to do.

Walt stared at the back of his hand.

Steady, he thought, steady. Try to relax. The shock . . . it's not fair . . . she knows so much. . . .

Study the room; think of something else. The ship; I'd like to see Calvin's face again. . . . There's my face — in the mirror. It looks all right.

Forential will be angry. I shouldn't have let her get away. I should have — what should I have done? Could I have?

I could have. . . .

He shook his head. No: that wouldn't have fooled her either.

Forential, what am I going to do now?

Walt sat down. He tried to think things out. I'm no good, he thought. The only thing I'm good for is to kill earthlings. I ought to be ashamed of myself.

. . . I'm alone, he thought. Things are going all wrong.

I've . . . I've got to learn to depend on myself.

I've always depended too much on Forential.

I've always been told what to do, he thought. It's time for me to begin telling myself what to do.

He nodded his head at the truth of this. I'm on my own, he thought. Well, by God, it's time to face that! I'll stop her some way.

Forential is depending on me!

At last it occurred to him to try to locate Julia. He concentrated. He formed Julia's pattern in his mind. He sought to equate it with reality. For a moment of bleak despair, he felt nothing. Then the pattern and reality overlapped. He fixed her in space. He had her. She was fleeing in an automobile.

And — she had changed! She was now — as she had been once before — as impotent as an earthling.

He sprang to his feet. Elation filled him. A rising tide of confidence swept over him.

Damn, damn, damn! he thought in excited delight. She's mine now!

Julia, oh Julia, can you hear me?

She couldn't.

He could feel her fleeing.

I'll show her now, he thought with savage satisfaction.

Wait'll I catch you!

There'll be no nonsense about privacy this time! he promised himself. I'll kill her where ever I find her. Forential may not like it as well as — to hell with Forential!

Outside the hotel, in the crisp, fresh night air, Walt plunged into the crowd emptying from a theater, whose marquee, "Junkeroo", flashed lonesomely above the sidewalk.

I'll need a car to overtake her, he thought.

He remembered back to his first ride. I can operate one, he thought, if I can start it. It's easy.

Julia lies in that direction. I'll catch her in no time.

He heard a car door open behind him.

He spun on his heel and walked back to the car. The driver, settled behind the wheel, was just depressing the light stud when Walt cut in front of it and came abreast of the driver's side.

"You're the one I'm looking for," he said.

"Eh?"

"Move over!"

The owner was a heavy, middle aged man; he snorted and narrowed his eyes. "What's this baloney?"

"I'm taking this car."

"The hell you say!"

Walt pulled the door open, grabbed the man by the shirt and twisted. He set his feet and the man came sprawling out into the street.

Holding him, Walt slapped his face.

The man flailed wildly. He tried to jerk loose. His shoulders twisted. He tried with a knee, and Walt threw him to the pavement. A few startled passers-by turned to watch.

Walt picked the man up and thrust him into the car. The man's face was purple with rage. He tried to scream.

Walt displaced the air from his lungs. The man collapsed, gagging.

"Don't make any loud noises," Walt said.

The man choked and gasped with suddenly restored breath.

". . . what . . . what do you want?"

"How do you start this car?"

The man started to protest; the look on Walt's face made him think better of it. He told Walt how to start the car.

Walt followed instructions. He listened to the purr of the motor.

"What is the power? What makes it run?"

The owner wiped blood from his face. Sullenly, through swelling lips, he said, ". . . it's a combustion engine . . . like all cars. . . ."

Cautiously maneuvering the car into traffic, Walt said, "Tell me what you know about combustion engines."

Walt displaced air again. He put it back. "I asked you to tell me what you know about combustion engines."

The man kept dabbing at his lips.

Gasping, the man began to explain. He did not seem too sure of himself. Every other sentence, he faltered, and Walt had to prompt him sharply.

"This fuel . . . this gas. . . . When the supply is used up, how does one obtain more?"

"From a . . . gas station. . . . "

I'll have to watch the fuel supply, Walt thought.

"They're . . . they're on nearly every corner," the man said.

Walt nodded. I've got all I can from him, he thought. "Do you have a small, heavy object?"

The man licked his cut lip. His eyes were wide with terror. "Y — ye — yes."

"Produce it!"

The man brought out a cigarette lighter.

Teleporting, Walt jerked it from the man's hand and hit him behind the ear with it. With a sigh, the owner collapsed unconscious.

I'm doing all right, Walt thought. Now, if I can just find the right road to follow.

He concentrated on Julia.

He began to drive very fast, slipping in and out of traffic recklessly.

Six blocks later, he picked up the police car.

And three blocks after that, the police car was abreast of him, forcing him to the curb.

Annoyed, Walt brought the car to a stop. The police car angled in ahead of him. Walt waited confidently.

"Okay," the policeman said wearily, taking out his book of tickets and putting one foot on the running board. "Where's the fire?"

Walt said, "Fire?"

"Yeah. The speed limit in this town is thirty miles an hour. Where's the fire? Let's see your license."

Walt considered this information. He removed the air from this policeman's lungs; from the lungs of the policeman in the car. When they were very unconscious, he let them have air again. He experimented with a few buttons until he found the reverse. He backed up a few yards, circled out around the police car, and continued. The policemen were still unconscious.

Mr. Green, the producer, stopped in front of the bank. With hurried thanks, Julia scrambled out.

Pathetically he called after her: "But we could —"

Inside the revolving doors, she pattered across the inlaid floor to the teller's cage still open for business. If I can just get out of here alive! she thought. The high, vaulted ceiling — dim and shadowy above the cool lights — seemed to echo her thoughts: get out of here alive, get out alive, alive.

She gave her name crisply and fumbled in her handbag for identification. "I want to withdraw my money."

"Yes, Miss. Your account is with this branch?"

"Yes." She handed her identification and her check book to him.

While she twisted nervously, he phoned to verify her account.

She could feel Walt creeping up on her. Her skin crawled. The revolving door was motionless.

That meant nothing. He could walk *through* it.

There was no easy way of telling how he would strike until the last moment. It would be so swift that she would never feel the blow at all.

She stared, fascinated, at the ink well across the room. She imagined it suddenly ripped out and hurled at her. She shivered. She tried to teleport it herself.

It did not move.

Cold sweat began to ooze from her pores. Brakes squealed in the street outside. She ran her hands along the carrying strap of her handbag. Her mouth was dry.

I'm too scared to spit! she thought. I've heard of that. I didn't believe it. It's true.

"For God's sake, hurry!"

"Yes, Miss," the teller said. He eyed her suspiciously.

How long can this go on? she thought despairingly. He'll be here in another minute!

"I have the amount. It's the same as your check stub shows," the teller said. "You want it all?"

"Yes."

"Just take this over to the table, there, and fill it in."

Oh, God! she thought.

She crossed to the table. Her hand was shaking. The free pen blotted. She ripped out the check and crumpled it into a ball. Her breathing was shallow. She found her own pen. Shakily she filled in another check.

The teller looked at it. He waved it dry. He held it up. "Just a, moment, Miss. I'd like to verify the signature."

Her nails dug into her palms. She moved her feet uneasily. She glanced toward the door.

She fumbled in her handbag for a cigarette. She found a stale pack, shook one out. She lit it with a safety match and extinguished the match with a nervous flick of her arm. She inhaled.

The invasion. For the first time since she'd left the hotel it reoccurred to her.

Oh, Lord! she thought. How much time before that! She dropped her cigarette and ground it out.

The clerk was bending over, comparing signatures.

I've got to do something about the invasion! I've got to tell somebody! But . . . but . . . how can I ever convince anyone?

They'd think I was crazy. They'd detain me for questioning. They'd lock me up. If they did, he could come upon me and I couldn't even run!

Her face was bloodless. If I had my powers back. . . .

She began to pace. Two steps one way; two steps back; two steps the other way.

I could . . . I could show them how to operate on a human to make the bridge; I could talk to a surgeon. . . .

Could I?

Her mind was fuzzy. It was no longer easy to remember. So many compartments were no longer available.

Do I remember how? You . . . you. . . . She concentrated with every fiber of her being.

"Your signature is shaky," the clerk said.

She whirled on him. Her lips trembled. She choked back hot words.

"I'm upset tonight," she said weakly.

He grunted.

If he catches me, she thought, *I'll be dead.* He'll kill me! I'll never be able to convince anyone then!

Hurry, hurry, hurry!

"How do you want the money?" the clerk asked.

"Any way! Any way!"

He began to count bills.

If I stand still, he'll catch me! she moaned to herself. Even now. . . .

She glanced toward the door.

"There," the clerk said.

Trembling, she stuffed bills into her handbag. She raced for the entrance and burst from the revolving doors. She cried out to the taxi idling across the street. The driver started the motor. She ran across the street to the car.

"Take me to a car lot that's open!"

"Yes, Lady."

She fumbled out a bill and threw it at him. She settled back in the seat. "Hurry!"

He looked at the bill. "Yes, indeed." He started the car. "I sure will."

The cab whirled away and U-turned toward Vermont.

She felt better to be moving.

And ten minutes later she was arguing with a salesman.

"This will do," she insisted. "I don't want a triple-guarantee, a road test, a service check, a —"

"I'll have to make out a bill of sale."

"All I want to know is: Is the gas tank full?"

Indignantly, the salesman said: "Of course."

"Mail me the bill of sale! Tear it up! I don't care! Here — Here's my hotel." After thrusting the card on him, she began to count money.

"The keys are in the ignition. I'll get your extra set. The license —" He began to recount the money.

She got behind the wheel, snapped on the lights, pressed the ignition button. The motor coughed and roared.

She spun the car out of the lot. She was weak with relief.

Maybe I can outrun him!

I hope.

I've got to!

I'll get as far away as I can. Then I'll . . . I'll have to take a chance waiting for an airplane. Then . . . then . . . when my money gives out. . . .

I can't hope to run forever.

She shuddered.

Walt crawled out of the wreck. It seemed to be a miracle he was unhurt.

He had switched the car to automatic drive as he had seen the driver on the desert do; he had not known that there was no automatic-drive beam on that particular stretch of highway.

At the first curve — in a heart beat of time; too fast for him to avert it — the car had hurtled the road and plowed into the embankment.

Walt cursed and shook his head and closed his eyes tightly, gathering his thoughts.

A few minutes later a car with intensely bright headlights stopped to give assistance. Walt threw the driver out and slipped behind the wheel.

In a moment he knew that he had a powerful motor under him.

VIII

An hour later (two of the twelve hours were gone) Julia was still free. She had weaved and twisted across the city. She had crossed and recrossed the super-highways and the local speedways. She had fled up ramps and through under passes.

She had no way of telling how near Walt was; or what moment and from what direction death might strike. She did not believe that he could reach out through space to snatch her life; if he tried teleportation, she was steeled to resist. The lifeless, glittering windows, the dull glare of overhead and curb lights, the shuttle movement of traffic, the heavy, motionless air — all these combined into bristling menace. Her foot strained against the accelerator; her muscles ached over the wheel.

She hoped she had confused him. Now she streamed for the

open highway. She settled the car into a traffic slot on the north-bound coast super-highway. She switched the car on automatic and tried to relax.

The road curved gently toward the west to pick up the coast line. Soon the moonlit breakers hissed on white sand beaches. The ocean lay dark and mysterious toward the far horizon.

She prayed that Walt would not guess for long minutes that she had left the city; that he would lose more precious minutes locating the super-highway.

San Francisco was six hours ahead of her.

Walt was continually losing himself in a maze of Los Angeles streets. Ones that seemed to promise to deliver him cross-town to interrupt Julia in her erratic course twined away in improper directions. Occasionally he neared her. But she darted away each time: as if with the primeval instinct of a hunted animal.

At last he stopped the car and cried to a pedestrian across the street: "Is there any place I can get a map of the city?"

"Ask inna filling station."

Walt snarled. And five minutes later he found the map. He memorized it carefully; it required scarcely more than a minute. During that time, he let his body rest and relax. He threw the map onto the driveway. He grew increasingly more confident of catching her as the information settled into his brain. He visualized the map.

He was ready for her now.

She was already on the super-highway. He left the filling station. He was in no hurry. He was waiting for her to return.

It soon became apparent that she would not.

He grunted and spun his car in her direction.

He lost several minutes in a traffic jam downtown. He got on the wrong lane in a clover leaf beyond the city limits. He had now passed beyond the boundaries of the map he had memorized. He took the ridge super-highway instead of the one Julia had taken. After twenty miles, he realized his mistake and had to cut over.

He bounced along an east-west road that was so rough-surfaced he had to reduce his speed.

When he finally arrived on the proper highway he was almost an hour behind Julia.

He concentrated on understanding the physical assembly of the engine in front of him. He could teleport parts from it; he could hold other parts more tightly together by using the same power. But the engine was so very complex. There was (he could tell) something there — in the engine itself — that kept the power from being utilized. He could not locate the block.

He increased the speed by tightening the valves. But the required concentration was too great to be long maintained. It exhausted him and forced him to rest for a few miles. Then he tightened the valves again. The car moved forward in a sudden burst of speed.

In San Francisco Julia stopped long enough for a sandwich — long enough to gulp hot coffee — long enough to buy a box of "Wide-awakes." She checked airline schedules by phone.

The eastern flights were held up by weather over the Rockies. The next strato-jet to Hawaii was due to leave in thirty minutes; but she would have to wait to see if any reservations were canceled before she could be assured of a seat. There would not be another plane south for an hour and a half. One was leaving just then.

She told herself that the airport would become a cul-de-sac unless she could time it perfectly; she could not risk it.

She cruised the city until she had been there over an hour. She was loggy and exhausted.

She was afraid to remain any longer. He might head her off; he might trap her in a dead end street. Once on the straight of way, there was — at least — no danger of that. She left the city and headed north again.

Walt arrived ten minutes before she left. He came to a stop at an all night lunch. Invisible, he slipped through walls into the kitchen. He stole food, returned to his car with it, ate it. He drove to a gas station, keeping her position sharply in mind.

"Gas," he ordered the attendant.

The attendant began filling the tank.

"All the way full," Walt said. "I want a map of the city when you finish."

The attendant brought the map. Walt unfolded it.

Julia had left the city. Walt was not going to be fooled this time. But he wanted to memorize the city just in case she did double back.

"Is there . . . a larger map? Of this whole area?"

The attendant brought him a California map. He memorized that one. He picked out Julia's route. He verified it.

"Pay up, now," the attendant said. "I gotta car waitin'. It's five sixty-seven altogether."

Walt reached through the rolled down window and seized the man. He jerked him forward and down; and, with the same motion, slammed his own weight against the inside of the unlocked door. The steel top of the opening door cracked the attendant across the forehead; he went limp. Walt let go of him. closed the door, and drove off.

By the time he sighted her car ahead of him on the highway, in the mist and fog of dawn, nearly eleven hours had elapsed since he had begun the pursuit. It had been only a half an hour before that he had located the governor and teleported it out of the engine.

IX

Julia saw the bright lights behind her. They blinded her in the rear-view mirror until she knocked the mirror out of focus. She glanced at the speedometer. She was going as fast as the engine would permit.

She was weary from the beat of the motor and the ache of steady driving. Her body was drained of energy. The "Wide-awakes" seemed to be losing their effect. In spite of herself, she nodded. Too tired to think of anything else, she was thinking — almost dreaming, almost in half-slumber — of a steamy bath; of perfumed heat caressing her body; of soft, restful water lapping at her thighs.

Even the prospect of invasion had receded into some dim, dumb corner of her mind; it no longer concerned her. The demands of personal survival had pushed it aside; personal survival and the knowledge of her own incapacity to prevent, forestall, or counter it. And at last exhaustion had overcome even the demands of survival.

The brilliant lights behind began to pain upon her fatigue-soaked eyeballs. They shimmered in the windshield; they —

She realized they were gaining on her.

A car without a governor.

A crazy, reckless driver.

Walt!

Suddenly the fatigue vanished. Fear alerted her. She stiffened. Her heart pounded. She glanced behind her, squinting.

There was a sickening wrench at her body; she felt herself twisting, being sucked out of space.

Teleportation!

She grabbed the wheel. She was almost too weak to resist. She fought off the terrible, insistant fingers, she shrank away from them; she moaned.

Walt ceased the effort.

She was limp. She struggled to marshal her resources. Her will was not yet depleted so much that she could not fight back.

She concentrated on being where she was, in the car, on the highway. She felt a futile but exhilarating surge of victory.

Her hand trembled when she switched off the automatic-drive. The wheel under her hands began to vibrate. The car was sensitive to her control. It was alive and deadly and hurtling like a rocket.

I can't outrun him now! she thought. He has too much speed!

. . . I've got to get off the highway. I've got to take a side road toward the mountain. There'll be curves and twists and turns. They will cut his speed down. Maybe I can out drive him.

Side roads slipped by to her right and left.

She prepared to brake the car for the next cut-off slot.

It appeared far ahead; a dark slit on the left outlined by her rushing headlights.

She depressed the brake; the tires screamed.

The car skittered and fishtailed. She clung desperately to the wheel, battling the great chunk of metal with every ounce of her tiny body.

And somehow the car hurtled through the slot, across the other half of the highway, onto the hard topped, farm-to-market road that climbed toward the distant crest.

Walt's car, braking shrilly, hurtled past her and was lost in the night.

Julia stamped the accelerator viciously. Her car plunged forward.

Lonely trees and brush stood like decaying phantoms in the splatter of her headlights. Far ahead, winking down the mountain, she saw the headlights of another car — crawling toward her slowly, like twin fire flies, indolent after a night of pleasure. The road was pitted, and the car beneath her jolted.

It was then in the loneliness of the seldom traveled farm road that she noticed the gasoline gauge.

The gas remaining in the tank could not be sufficient to take her another ten miles. The peg rested solidly on the empty mark to the left.

She began to cry. The tears almost blinded her; she jerked the car back, just in time, from a ditch. She held it toward the fearful darkness ahead. Dawn that purpled the east seemed lost forever from this road and this life.

The road climbed slowly; then steeply.

Behind her now the bright lights like great flames crept closer, burning everything. The lights had pursued her for only half an hour; it seemed an eternity. The road began a great bend around the first sharp thrust of mountain. She slowed.

The headlights were gaining.

She wanted to give up.

The motor coughed.

Walt was almost upon her; elation throbbed in his being. He had been driving on manual; he dared not risk automatic-drive, not since his wreck. He was not quite as alert as he might have been. The strain was beginning to slow his reactions.

The curve was sharper; ahead, a hair-pin turn. Walt swung out to pass her and force her to stop or plunge over the side into the deepening valley. It was the maneuver he had seen the policemen perform.

The headlights of the early farmer with a heavy load of milk suddenly exploded at the curve.

Julia gasped and slammed on her brakes.

Walt jerked his eyes from Julia's car an instant before the crash.

"Crazy God damned fool," the farmer said as he crawled painfully from the wreckage of his pickup truck. "Crazy God damned fool!" He clutched at his arm; it was broken and bleeding. "Passing on a curve! God damned fool, passing on a curve!"

Julia had stopped her car. She ran toward the two wrecks.

"Any kid knows better, any two year old kid," the farmer said; he stared, unbelieving, at his arm. He sat down and was sick.

It was growing lighter. Mist lay over the valley. The air was damp with fading night.

Julia's feet made harsh clicks on the road.

At Walt's car she stopped. The farmer watched her with mute pain behind his eyes.

Reaction set in. She thought she was going to be sick, herself. She leaned against the wrecked car.

"We better get him out," the farmer said dully.

Julia nodded.

Between the two of them, they forced the door open and lifted Walt out to the pavement.

"Easy," the farmer said.

Julia stood over Walt's limp body. His jaw was broken and twisted to one side. His chest was bloody; blood trickled from his nose; his hair was matted with blood.

"He's still breathing," the farmer said hoarsely.

He looks so boyish, she thought. I can't believe . . . he doesn't seem a killer. I hate whoever made a killer out of him.

Walt's chest rose and fell; his breath entered his body in tremulous gasps.

She wanted to bathe his face with cool water and rest his head on her lap. She wanted to ease his pain.

She turned away.

In the tool compartment of the wreck she located a tire iron. She brought it back.

Her hand was slippery around the icy metal.

He's dying anyway, she thought. It doesn't have to be my hand that kills him. Tears formed in her eyes.

Walt moaned.

Julia's hand tightened on the tire iron.

But the risk . . . she thought: if he should wake up and heal himself . . . he'll kill me. The world will never be warned of the invasion, then. It's his life against the world; his life against a billion lives.

She lifted the tire iron. She averted her eyes as she got ready to swing it savagely at his unprotected skull.

Cursing, the farmer reached out with his good hand and grabbed her upraised wrist. "My God, what are you trying to do?"

"I've . . . I've got to kill him."

The farmer stepped between her and Walt.

"I've got to."

"Not while I'm here, Miss, you don't."

"Listen — !" she began. Then hopelessly, she let the arm holding the tire iron fall limply to her side. He wouldn't believe me if I told him, she thought.

Nobody will believe me; not a person on the planet. It's too fantastic: an invasion of earth. I've got to have some sort of proof to make them believe me.

No proof.

I can't let Walt die! she thought. He's the only proof I have. He's the only one who can convince anyone of the invasion.

He's *got* to live! she thought. I've got to get him to a hospital.

Walt's face was bloodless.

". . . he's dying," the farmer said.

"But he can't die!" Julia cried desperately. "He can't die!"

"You're crazy," the farmer said evenly. "First you get ready to brain him with a tire iron and then you say he's got to live. Lady, if I hadn't stopped you when I did, he'd be dead as hell right now."

"I wasn't thinking; I didn't realize. . . ."

Breath rattled in Walt's throat.

"Gas . . . I'm out of gas," Julia said.

She ran to the wrecked truck. She jerked a milk can upright. She unscrewed the cap and emptied milk on the pavement.

With the tire iron she split the gas tank and caught as much of the sharp-smelling fluid as she could in the emptied can.

It sloshed loudly as she raced to her car with it. She fumbled the gas tank cap off. She was trembling so badly that she spilled almost as much as she poured into the opening. When the gas was all gone, she threw the milk can from her.

"I'll back up!" she cried to the farmer. "You'll have to help me get him into the back seat."

He's got to live, Julia thought. If the doctors can just bring him to consciousness, he can heal himself. When he realizes I've saved his life, maybe he'll listen to me. He's got to listen. I'll convince him, I'll reason with him. He'll be able to prove to everybody that there will be an invasion. When they see all the things he can do, they'll have to believe him. . . .

They put Walt in the car. They handled him as gently as they could.

"He's almost gone," the farmer said.

"Get in front with me. You need a hospital, too."

The farmer slipped in beside her.

Julia spun the car around and plunged down the road toward the super-highway.

"Where's the nearest doctor?"

"Town eight miles down the road," the farmer said. He grimaced in pain. He coughed, and blood flecked his lips. He wiped off the blood and stared at it drying across the back of his hand. "I . . . think I'm hurt inside." There was barely controlled hysteria in his voice. He coughed again and shuddered. "My wife, she wanted me . . . to stay home this morning. . . ." He shut his eyes tightly. "I've got to patch the roof." He opened his eyes and looked pleadingly at Julia. *"I've got to patch the roof, don't you understand!"*

"I'm driving as fast as I can. Which way do I turn down there?"

". . . turn right."

"We'll be to a doctor just as soon as I can get there."

She slowed down and turned onto the concrete slab of the super-highway.

Then she slammed the car to a full stop; she backed up out of the line of traffic, back onto the cross road. She cut the motor.

Julia had felt the bridge in her mind snap shut. Instantly even the most obscure brain compartment was open to her. Fatigue vanished. She was alert; she was able to think with great clarity.

The lightning recovery of *herself* forced a series of ever widening implications to her attention; in a blinding flash of insight she was (perhaps actually for the first time) aware of the degree to which she could transform society.

Given time, she — she alone — like the magician Prospero in *The Tempest* could create some paradise of cloud-capped towers and gorgeous palaces and solemn temples and winding brooks and crisp channels and green lands that need never (the Calibans being transmuted by power beyond the lust for power) dissolve into air, thin air, leaving not a cloud behind.

If all the people were as she, the great globe of the world could become an enchanted island: with wars and bloodshed and prejudice and inhumanity forgotten.

Some such was her thought. It washed over her, the vision, and vanished in the acute reality of the moment. Such a dream was athwart the invasion plan of the aliens.

She was out of the car. She was opening the rear door. She stood at Walt's head. He'll have to help me, she thought, he has information I want.

She felt for the pattern of his body. She experienced it. Concentrating with the full force of the human brain, she began to mend the breaks and ruptures and wounds.

It took time.

Don't reheal his mutant bridge, she thought. Leave him defanged.

His jaw returned to its socket. The dried blood on his skin no longer led from vicious gashes: they had closed and were knitting.

She was finished. He was still unconscious.

Even as she turned to heal the farmer, a section of her brain drew conclusions from the fact she could be relieved of her powers. Some outside force was responsible for holding the bridge closed in her mind. It could be turned on and off.

But why, when the force controlling her bridge had vanished, had Walt's bridge remained intact? She reviewed all the information she had.

There are two compartments of mutants on the alien ship.

Then each compartment must have its own . . . frequency. The aliens selected Walt, she thought, to kill me because his bridge operated on a different frequency than mine.

Speechless the farmer had watched her heal Walt; now he relaxed under the soothing fingers of her thought. He felt the bone in his arm being made whole again.

He no longer needed to cough.

She tried to create a bridge in his brain; but she could not; it was outside the pattern. If she were to give him one, it would require surgery.

She was once again in the seat beside him.

"You're a, you're an *angel*," he said. Awe made his voice hollow. "I'll be God damned if you're not an honest to Jesus, real live angel."

"I'm human."

". . . you couldn't be."

"Well, I am."

He frowned. ". . . lady, after what I just seen you do, I'll believe it if you say so. You just tell me, I'll believe it."

"I've got to get into San Francisco. I'll have to leave you. You can catch a ride or something."

He scrambled out of the car.

Impulsively Julia reached in her handbag for a bill. She found one. "Here", she said, thrusting it on him, "this is for your milk."

The farmer took it automatically. He put it in his wallet and put the wallet back in his overalls without bothering to watch what he was doing. He was watching her.

If they're all as easy to convert as he is . . . she thought.

"Can I ask you a question?"

"What?" she said.

"If you're human, what am I?"

"We're not *quite* the same," Julia said. "Maybe some day we will be. . . ."

She wheeled onto the super-highway and headed toward San Francisco.

She switched on the automatic-drive and turned her attention to Walt.

She was unable to awaken him. After such a severe shock as he had experienced, his nervous system demanded rest; he no longer had the recuperative powers of a mutant.

Even if I alert Earth, she thought what can we *do*? How can we prepare? I could . . . but I'm only one. They'd gang up on me and kill me in a minute. . . . Earth will fight; at least we won't give up. I'll have to get us as ready as I can, and we'll fight.

I need Walt. What kind of weapons will we be up against? Where will the invasion strike first? When? He'll have scraps of information that I can put together to tell me more than he thinks he knows.

How can I convince him to help me?

. . . if I've figured it out right, there's got to be records somewhere. Birth certificates, things like that. If I'm right about babies being missing the year of the last big saucer scare, there's got to be birth certificates. I'll check newspaper files in San Francisco.

If I can just find Walt's birth certificate! That will convince him!

She thought about the space station floating somewhere in the sky; she tried to picture the aliens who manned it.

God knows how, she thought, but we'll fight!

* * * *

In the space station, the aliens were in conference.

★★There can't be any doubt but that she's dead,★★ Forential projected.

★★Your Walt is a good one,★★ Lycan thought. ★★Best mutant on the ship.★★

Jubilation flowed back and forth. The other aliens congratulated Forential.

★★It was nothing,★★ Forential told them.

★★I feel infinitely better, now that she's out of the way,★★ the Elder commented.

★★We'll strike with the main force a day before we planned to,★★ Lycan told them. ★★That's best all around. We expect most trouble from the American Air Force. It will be least alert on a Sunday morning.★★

In San Francisco, Julia drew up in front of an unpretentious hotel on Polk Street. Walt was still unconscious in the back seat.

After she arranged for a room, she returned to the car. She seized Walt at his arm pits and hauled him to the sidewalk. She held a tight distortion field around his body. He was dead weight against her. She draped one of his arms about her neck. When she began to walk, his feet shuffled awkwardly.

She felt as conspicuous, as if she were smoking a pipe.

She wedged her body against the door of the hotel and dragged Walt inside. Although he was invisible, the effect of his body pulling down on hers was readily apparent. She half stumbled toward the elevator.

The clerk, a counterpart of the one she had had in Hollywood looked up in annoyance. He snorted through his nose. He eyed her narrowly. He seemed about to leave his position behind the desk.

Julia propped Walt against the wall and rang for the elevator. She smiled wanly in the direction of the clerk. Shaking his head and grunting his disapproval, he settled back in his chair.

Walt's heavy breathing was thunderous in her ear. She braced him with her hip when he started to slip to the floor.

The elevator came.

"Step up, please."

Straining against his weight, she hauled Walt's feet up over the edge of the cage. The feet scraped loudly on the floor.

The elevator operator raised his eyebrows ever so slightly. He cocked his head to one side. "Something wrong?"

"Oh, no," Julia said brightly. "Everything's fine."

The operator started the car. "A young lady ought to be careful in this town," he said. "A young lady oughtn't to drink so much." He shook his head sadly. "There's a case of rape in the papers nearly every day."

". . . I'll be careful."

"They pick up young ladies in bars all the time. You never can tell about the men you're liable to meet, if you go in bars. You have to watch yourself in this town."

"Seven, please."

"Yes, ma'm."

The elevator stopped. Julia dragged Walt out.

"You mind what I say!" the operator called after her. "You be careful, now, and stay out of bars. You never can tell. . . . "

Once she got Walt inside her room, she breathed a sigh of relief. She released the distortion field. He was visible again.

She removed the top sheet from the bed. She wrestled his body onto the bed.

She ripped the sheet into strips. She worked rapidly. She was still able to hold off fatigue; she felt no need of sleep. She was ravenously hungry.

With the strips of sheet, she tied Walt securely. She used a knot that would require cutting to be undone. She pulled the strips tight. They did not interfere with free circulation, but there was no possibility of them being slipped. She had no intention of not finding Walt there when she came back.

She surveyed her handiwork with satisfaction.

Whistling softly she left the room and walked down the corridor. She stopped whistling abruptly and glanced around in embarrassment. She had remembered the old adage: 'A whistling girl and a crowing hen are sure to come to some bad end'.

There seemed to be something *indecent* about whistling in public.

The fact that she had, colored her emotions with uneasiness.

She realized that there might be a million such superstitions — many of them not recognized as superstitions at all — buried in her personality. Her brain might be highly efficient, but was it efficient enough to overcome all the emotional biases implanted by twenty-four years of environment? Was even her knowledge of the real nature of the world — was mankind's — sufficient to overcome such biases?

Perhaps, she thought, I'm not as smart as I thought I was. There may be deep and illogical currents in me. Perhaps I'm not, not *mature* enough for such power as I've been given.

Annoyed, she took out a cigarette, and in defiance of cultural tradition, lit it there in the corridor while she waited for the elevator.

The operator did not approve of women smoking in public. He said so.

She ate in the coffee shop.

After the meal, she took a cab to the offices of the morning paper.

In the entranceway to the building, sure that no one was watching, she became invisible.

Half an hour later, possessed of the information she had come after (harvested from the back files of the paper) she was once again in the street.

In her room, she went to the telephone. She placed a long distance call to a Boston hospital.

The news had not been widely reported. She found most of the names in brief paragraphs stating that Mr. and Mrs. such and such had settled their suit against the so and so hospital out of court. In the three cases where the confinements had been in private homes, there had been kidnapping stories in the paper. In one of the cases, a man had later been convicted and executed — although the body of the child had never been recovered from the pond into which the prosecution contended it had been thrown.

She talked to the switch board operator at the Boston hospital. She was given the superintendent. He — impressed by the fact that she was calling from the Pacific coast — sent his secretary to rummage the files for the hospital's copy of the birth certificate.

Julia waited.

"Yes, I have it."

"It's on the child of Mr. and Mrs. George Temple?"

"That's right."

Julia concentrated as hard as she could.

"You have it in your hand?"

"Yes."

"Would you look at it closely?"

"... what?"

"Look at it closely, please."

"Young lady —"

"*Please*, sir."

"All right. I am. Now what information did you want? It reads — What the hell! Where did that go? Say, how did you —"

Julia hung up. She looked at the birth certificate lying by the telephone. She picked it up. It was none the worse for teleportation.

She put it on the dresser and returned to the phone.

By the time Tuesday was well into the afternoon, when the cool rays of the winter sun lay slanting upon the murmuring crest outside, she had nine birth certificates on the dresser. Nine times the bell boy had come to her room to collect for the telephone charges. The last time, she forgot to make Walt invisible. The bell boy said nothing.

Julia was annoyed by her carelessness. The bell boy's footfalls died in the carpet of the corridor. She went to the door and looked out. He was gone.

She closed the door and crossed to the bed. She had exhausted her list of names. She set about rousing Walt.

He's handsome, she thought.

His eyelids flickered.

He opened his eyes. Memory slowly darkened his irises. He glared up at her.

He surged at his bonds, striving to rip free and throw himself upon her. He tugged at his right hand. His fingers writhed. A frown passed over his face. He jerked his right hand savagely.

"You have been deprived of your power," Julia said.

Stunned, he lay back. "I, I don't understand."

"You thought you were a Lyrian," Julia said. "You were wrong. You're an earthman. I am an earthwoman."

"That's a lie! I'm not an earthman!"

"You are now. How are you different?"

"That's a lie. I'm, I'm. . . ." He fought against the tentacle-like strips of sheet.

"Is it a lie, Walt?"

He continued to struggle.

Smiling, she taunted him: "When I was a little girl, I used to get mad and throw rocks. . . . It never did any good. Lie still."

I shouldn't tease him, she thought contritely.

She felt very sorry for him. How frustrated he must feel! How hurt and puzzled and helpless and betrayed!

He's like Samson shorn.

"I know how you feel," she said softly. "I felt that way when you were chasing me. You're going to listen to me. After I'm through talking to you, maybe I'll let you up."

Glaring hotly, he relaxed.

"I saved your life," Julia said. "Don't forget that. You could thank me."

"You had a reason then. You're a traitor. You had your reasons to."

She slipped to the end of the bed. Gently she unlaced his shoes and slipped them off.

His face purpled with impotent anger.

She peeled off his socks.

Then, one by one, Julia compared the footprints on the birth certificates with Walt's feet.

Hot tears of defeat brimmed up within Walt; indignant rage filled his eyes.

Julia turned to put the birth certificates back on the dresser. None of them corresponded to his prints.

Walt wanted to bite down on something. He gritted his teeth. Then, as Julia was turning away from him, he felt once again the weird blending of his mind with Calvin's. He realized that it was some exclusive power given to Calvin that caused the blending: he was not even any longer a, a Lyrian!

Joy vibrated in his body. Drawing on the new power in his mind, he hurled a picture from the wall at the back of Julia's unprotected head.

She half turned. The heavy wooden frame hit her in the temple. With a little despairing sigh of surprise she sank to the carpet.

I'll kill her this time, Walt thought. He displaced the binding from his right hand.

And Calvin's mind withdrew.

Walt tried desperately to tear loose his other hand; the knot would not yield. He tried to reach Julia. He tried to reach something to throw at Julia. He could not. He let out a roar of baffled rage.

Julia was struggling to her feet.

Standing uncertainly, she shook her head. Her eyes cleared. She let out her breath. The recuperative powers of a mutant were in action. "That was an awful wallop," she said calmly. "How did you manage it?"

Walt said nothing.

Julia wrinkled her forehead. Her mind was steady and alert. "I felt another mind just before I turned. Someone called Calvin, wasn't it?"

Walt was sweating. *How smart is she? Can she guess everything?*

"Somehow he gains rapport with you." Her fingers tapped restlessly on the dresser top. "If you could maintain contact with his mind all the time, you would; that's obvious, isn't it? He must make contact with yours, then. You don't know just when he's going to contact you, do you?"

Walt licked his lips.

"He must be abnormal. A normal mutant couldn't do that. I'll have to find some way to seal his mind off from yours, I guess. I'll have to interfere with that sort of thing. In the meantime, I'll have to keep a sharp eye on you."

Walt glared at her. "Damn you," he said.

"Why don't the aliens do the fighting for themselves?"

The question was unexpected. "You got it wrong," he said automatically. "They are helping Lyrians out of the goodness of their hearts." It was as if he were speaking to Calvin; it made him feel, momentarily, superior to her. He grasped the opportunity with pathetic gratefulness. "They're afraid!" he cried triumphantly. "We're not that far advanced yet!"

Julia paused to consider this. "Yes, that figures," she said. "But suppose for a minute that you're not a Lyrian. Suppose they're using you to fight for *them*."

"No," Walt said.

"But why not?"

"No," he repeated. He tried to keep doubt out of his voice. His anger was gone. He felt uncertain and confused. He could not think clearly.

"You're a mutant," Julia said. "Like I am. Our parents were earthlings. The aliens are using mutants. The aliens changed our parents' genes —"

"I don't understand that word."

Julia smiled twistedly. "Think how ignorant they kept you, Walt. Isn't that proof enough for you?"

Walt said nothing.

". . . Genes are the substances which transmit characteristics from generation to generation. If you wish to change hereditary characteristics, you must change the genes. The aliens changed our genes so we would be able to use all of our brains. The normal earthling is just like you are right now: unable to use more than one sixth of his brain. The aliens collected all the mutants; all of them but me. They overlooked me."

Walt twisted uncomfortably.

"But they still control us," Julia said. "There is a bridge that is held closed by a special frequency. That's why we've just recently been able to use our full powers. They just recently turned the frequency on."

"But —"

"The frequency that controls my bridge is different from the one controlling yours. There are two groups of mutants on the ship. The female you saw, the one you thought was a Lyrian, was a mutant from the other group. I'm on the frequency of that group. It's the group that's going to attack Earth first. They are the ones that are going to cause the war your Forential told you about."

Walt's mouth was dry. Stop! he wanted to cry to her. Please, stop!

". . . keep birth records," Julia continued. Walt had missed some of it. "No two sets of prints can be identical. A group of babies vanished during the last big flying saucer scare. *You were one of them.* I was trying to find your birth certificate. If I could find it. . . ."

Julia talked on. Her voice was sincere and intense and compelling. As he listened, Walt felt the case against the aliens grow stronger.

Can't think clearly, he told himself. Trust Forential.

No.

He did lie about the war.

Forential lied about that.

He'd lie about . . . about other things?

They kept me in ignorance, he thought. Perhaps they really were afraid I'd discover my real nature.

I don't know; I can't think; I can't *think!*

As he watched Julia, the female who had (the truth of this slowly dawned on him) actually saved his life, he felt the first stirrings of an emotion he was not prepared to cope with. How pretty she looked, standing before him, her eyes serious and her face intent. He wanted to nestle her.

The footprints, he thought. She couldn't find mine among the birth certificates she had. She could have faked a set if she'd wanted to. Does the fact she didn't mean she's not lying?

I think I'm sorry I threw the picture at her.

"If you could have heard Mrs. Savage on the phone," Julia said, "you'd understand better. She lost her son — had him *stolen* — and she was still saving the birth certificate, after this long. She told me she knew she'd find him some day."

Mrs. Savage sounds just like Forential, Walt thought.

"She's been waiting all these years," Julia said. "She's never given up hope."

Still waiting for her . . . son, Walt thought. Still waiting, still needing her son.

Walt had never thought much of his parents until now. They were obscured by Forential; they existed somewhere on Lyria. But suppose Julia were telling the truth? Would they have been more fond of him than Forential? Could they have been?

There were so many things he did not understand. He must ask Forential about the process by which babies are created; what was the connection between parent and child? It was all so *puzzling*.

. . . why not ask Julia?

"Wait a minute," Walt interrupted. "I understand so very little. How are babies made?"

And there was a harsh, peremptory knock on the door. The manager's angry voice came booming through the paneling:

"The bell boy tells me you've got a man tied to the bed in there! We can't have that sort of thing in this hotel! Open the door, you hear me? Open the door!"

X

"Oh, oh," Julia whispered. "You keep your mouth shut, Walt."

She projected a distortion field around him.

The bed now appeared untenanted.

Walt was silent.

Julia opened the door. The manager stormed in.

"You, you creature!" he cried. "Tying a defenseless man on the bed for God knows what evil pur — oh. Hummm." he stared at the bed.

"Oh," he said.

"There's no one here but me."

"The bell boy —"

The manager searched the room. He looked in the closet. He looked in the shower. His face slowly began to take on color.

Foolishly he got down on his knees and peered under the bed.

"Well," he said, dusting off his trousers as he stood up, "well . . . oh. . . . Is the service all right, Miss? Do you have any complaints? Plenty of towels? Soap? Did the bell boy raise the window — yes, I see he did. There's enough heat? I, I seemed to have — I was on the wrong floor entirely. You see —"

His face grew even more puzzled. "There's a woman on the, on the *ninth* floor I guess it is — how could I ever have made such a mistake? this is the seventh floor, isn't it? — has a man in her bed." His face got redder. He waved his hands. "Tied to the bed."

"Oh, my," Julia said.

"Yes, isn't it. Now, if you want anything, don't hesitate to ring. I'm sorry about this mistake. Silly of me. This is the *seventh* floor . . . isn't it?"

"Yes, this is the seventh floor."

The manager left.

Julia locked the door behind him.

She dissolved the distortion field.

"Whew!" she said. "He was mad, wasn't he?"

Walt tried to sit up.

"No — wait. I think I'll take a chance. I'm going to leave you alone to think over what I've said. Then I'm going to come back and untie you. You're going to help me, Walt."

"I, I don't know what to think."

"Here's one thing I want you to remember when you're thinking everything out. *People can be convinced of anything as long as they have no way of checking beliefs against facts.* Remember that. Forential had complete control over you. You believed what he told you to. Now you've had a chance to see for yourself. You're just like an earthling. There is no war. Things like that. Think for yourself, Walt."

"How long will you be gone?"

Julia gathered up her handbag. She folded the birth certificates and stored them in it. "I don't know. I've got to convince someone of some facts that are going to be very hard to believe." She paused at the door. "I won't forget you, Walt. I'll be back soon." She smiled almost shyly. "If Calvin contacts you again, don't go away. I'll just have to hunt you down."

After she had gone, Walt relaxed. His body was still weak. He lay staring at the ceiling. Outside, the sun's rays slanted even more. A breeze, chill with approaching night, rustled the curtain.

There were shadows along the far wall.

I've been an instrument, Walt thought, a piece of metal, to be used as Forential saw fit: if she were not lying. My parents are somewhere down here on this planet, the third from the sun. They are not on Lyria. I might have killed them during the invasion. That would be worse than killing Forential, even. If Julia weren't lying to me. Forential has been raising me to fight my own people!

Forential. Saucer eyed. Tentacled. Moist and slippery. Breathing in labored gasps under high gravity. Air bubbling in his throat. Tentacles caressing, fondling — not with affection (if Julia is right) but with calculating design: to fashion my personality to his purpose. . . .

Walt closed his eyes.

Forential, he thought.

Forential was far away in space; every second he was growing farther away in time. I've lost him, Walt thought. So much has happened, so much, so fast, since last I saw him, that I'm changing away from him every minute.

Earthlings aren't so bad. They're — they're not too much different from Lyrians, from . . . *mutants.*

I'm a mutant?

I'm not a Lyrian?

FORENTIAL!

But Forential could not hear him.

I'll have to think for myself, Walt decided. Julia said I couldn't be fooled if I just looked at the facts.

Earthlings aren't like Forential always told us they were. They're pleasant enough. In their way. I don't see how they can menace Lyria (if there is such a place). *I don't think they've even got space travel!*

He tossed restlessly on the bed.

And Julia, he thought. Well, she's nice. She's all right.

She's. . . .

Again the new emotion troubled him. He missed her. He wished she would hurry back.

Julia!

. . . and why *did* she lose her powers if she's a Lyrian? Why did I? Lyrians shouldn't lose their powers.

What about the machines on the ship?

Can there really be another compartment of — mutants?

Is that why the walls of the ship were impenetrable?

Is that why we were never permitted in more than a fraction of the overall space of the ship?

I don't think, I don't think I like Forential any more.

Julia consulted a phone directory for the address of the local F. B. I. office.

It was four thirty when she arrived, and only one man was still in the office. He had his feet propped up on the desk; he was smoking a pipe and reading a law book.

"Yes?" he said, standing up as Julia came forward.

"You better sit back down," she said.

"Well, now. . . . And who are you?" He said it not unkindly.

Julia gave her name. Gravely he shook hands with her.

"Sit over there, Julia," he said.

When she was seated, he sat down. He bent forward and cleared his throat.

Oh, dear, how can I start? she thought. How can I ever start? "What, what was the page you were reading in your book?"

He ignored the question. His eyelids drooped wearily. He took out a notebook. He unscrewed his pen cap.

"I suppose you want to report on the family next door?" he

said.

"Well, as a matter of fact, no," Julia said. "I wanted —" And again her resolve faltered.

"Yes?" the F.B.I. man asked.

His law book floated from the table behind him and drifted over his shoulder. It opened itself before his face. The pages riffled.

"What page?" Julia asked intently.

The F.B.I. man took his pipe out of his mouth and looked at it. "Page one hundred and fifteen," he said.

The book fell open to that page.

The F.B.I. man plucked it out of the air. He felt all around it. He put it in his lap. His eyelids were no longer weary.

"I think I underestimated you," he said. "I believe I'm going to sit right here and take down every word you say." He gestured with his pipe. "Start talking."

Julia spoke slowly. She gave the F.B.I. man all the information she had. His pen skimmed rapidly, making short hand squiggles over the white pages of his notebook.

When she had finished, he looked up. He tossed the law book toward the desk. She caught it and let it down gently, so that it landed without a sound.

"Julia," the man said, "put yourself in my position. What would you do if someone came to you with a story like this?"

"I'd send that person to Washington, where she could talk to somebody."

"I'd like a little more proof."

Julia passed her hand through the back of the chair. "I should certainly be investigated: just on the basis of being able to do that, shouldn't I?"

The F.B.I. man nodded. "Do that again."

Julia did.

"Excuse me a minute," he said. He swiveled to his desk. He picked up his phone and dialed. He waited.

". . . Peggy? This is me. I won't be home for dinner tonight. A case just came in. . . ." He hung up.

He turned back to Julia.

"Now, about this space station. How is it we haven't seen it?"

"I assume it has a distortion field around it. It's invisible."

"Hummmm." He entered that in his notebook. "Is there any way we could detect it?"

"I. . . . If I were able to talk to a physicist, he might be able to build detection equipment. It would take time."

"I see. Now, about this Walt. How dangerous would you say he is?"

"I disconnected the bridge in his mind."

"Bridge?"

"I call it that. It's what makes us different. It could be built into a normal human being, I think."

"You mean," he said, "I could be fixed up to do the things you can do? Teleportation? Telepathy?"

"If I were a surgeon, I think I could change your brain to our pattern. I can see how it should be done. But I'd have to train to be able to. Surgery is a skill; it takes practice to master it."

"How long?"

"I don't know."

"How long until the invasion?"

"I don't know that either. I don't know whether or not I can find out from Walt. I doubt if he has enough information to tell me. Very soon now. Less than a month. Maybe even tomorrow."

"There's no time, then," he said. He chewed his lip. "I see. . . . The Air Force still has its saucer files. I'm going to refer you to it."

"We haven't much time. Remember that."

The F.B.I. man looked at his watch. "There's a plane to Washington in three hours. I'll get you reservations on it. I'll phone the head office there. There'll be somebody from the Air Force to meet you."

"I'll leave at eight, is that right?"

"From the city airport. Just a minute. I'm going to assign a man to you. I don't want anything happening between now and then."

"I can look out for myself," Julia said. "I'll pick up my ticket and Walt's at the reservation booth. 'Bye."

The F.B.I. man blinked his eyes. She had vanished. He got up and searched the office carefully. The door had not opened.

But she was gone.

Sweating, he went to the phone.

In less than two minutes, he was talking to Washington. When he recradled the phone, he was shaking. He took out his pipe, filled it, lit it, walked to the window.

He looked out at the twilight city. A lone star sparkled in the sky. He stared upwards.

"My God," he said softly to himself.

He crossed to the teletype, switched the current on. He began typing his notes on it for the benefit of Washington.

Back in the hotel room, Julia released Walt. Free, he stood up uncertainly.

"I think you'll help me," she said levelly. "I disconnected the bridge in your mind; I'm going to leave it that way. I can't afford not to. But am I right, Walt?"

"I'm not sure. I, I'll have to see."

"We're going to fly to Washington tonight."

"Washington?"

"The seat of the government. You clean up in the bathroom, now. But hurry. We'll have to catch a plane out of here at eight o'clock. It's after six."

"All right."

While she was waiting, she studied herself despairingly in the mirror. I look, she thought, like something the cat dug up.

When Walt came back, she took his arm possessively.

"I'm hungry," he said.

"Oh?" Julia said. "We'll have time to eat, I guess. I wish we didn't have to eat hotel food, though. I'm a good cook." She led Walt to the door. "You'll see what I mean, if we can get this invasion stopped. I'm going to make you invisible, now."

After they ate, Julia drove her car to the airport. The reservations were waiting. So was the F.B.I. man.

"I teletyped my report to them. They wanted me to accompany you."

He introduced himself to Walt.

Walt shook his hand. Walt no longer recoiled from the touch of an earthling.

In the plane, the F.B.I. man ordered cocktails. Walt had never tasted alcohol before. It was an unpleasant taste. But once it was down, it was not objectionable.

He forced himself to drain the glass. He felt himself relaxing.

"Ugh," he said.

The F.B.I. man ordered another round. Julia declined. Walt accepted.

Walt said, "I feel *warm.*"

The F.B.I. man kept glancing out the window of the plane, up at the stars. Clouds hung below; moonlight played over them.

Walt found that he was very . . . fond . . . of Julia. If only, he thought, she weren't so damned superior!

The alcohol filtered through his body. The compartment of the airplane danced not unpleasantly. He longed to feel Julia very close to him. He wanted to reach out and touch her uncovered skin.

Faintly, far off, barely heard was the sound of the others talking.

He grew heavy and sleepy. He closed his eyes.

He awakened once, and Julia was not beside him. He moved his tongue. It felt fuzzy and thick.

He wanted Julia.

"Julia!" he cried.

"I'm just up here," she called softly.

Disturbed passengers muttered their annoyance.

The stewardess came to Walt's seat.

"I don't want you!" Walt said. "Julia!" he shouted.

Julia came back to him.

"Sit down beside me," he commanded. And when she did, he went promptly back to sleep.

It was after three o'clock Wednesday morning when their plane set down wheels on the Washington airport runway.

A sleepy-eyed Air Force colonel was waiting at the gate. The F.B.I. man approached him. "Here they are."

"Okay."

The colonel crossed to them. "You're to come along with me."

"All right."

Walt shook his head to clear the sleep from his eyes.

They followed the colonel to the waiting, olive drab passenger car. The F.B.I. man had departed.

The colonel helped Julia in.

"We've got rooms for you downtown."

"Whatever you've decided," Julia said.

The colonel gave his driver the address.

Half an hour later, Julia and Walt and the colonel reached their destination.

"I must be a mess," Julia apologized. "I haven't had time to change clothes or anything."

"I'll order you some," the colonel said.

They went immediately to the third floor.

"This is your room," the colonel told Walt, opening the door.

"I want to stay with Julia," Walt said.

"This is your room," the colonel said stiffly. He signaled the guard lounging at the end of the corridor. The guard came.

"This is your man," the colonel told the guard.

The guard nodded.

"He's not to leave."

Walt planted his feet. "I'm not —"

"Go on in, Walt," Julia said.

Walt hesitated.

"Go on."

Reluctantly, Walt entered the room. The guard pulled the door closed.

"You're to come here," the colonel said. He led the way.

Once in her room, he said, "I know you're tired. . . ."

Julia realized that she was tired. Even her mutant powers could not keep fatigue out of her body forever. Her muscles ached. The strain and excitement had sapped her energy to a greater extent than she had realized.

"I am, a little. A few hours rest —"

"Would you sign this first?" the colonel asked. "It's a transcript of your conversation with the F.B.I. man. To make it official. It's all we need for the moment."

Julia flipped through it. It was very accurate.

The colonel produced a pen.

Julia signed.

"Now, one last thing. What sort of clothing did you want? I'll have my secretary buy the things in the morning."

Using hotel stationery, Julia made a list.

The colonel took it. "We'll call you in sometime tomorrow morning to get your testimony."

"I better give you some money for the list."

The colonel smiled. "You're a guest of the Air Force. We'll take care of it." At the door he said, "Oh, by the way, don't try to leave this room."

He closed the door softly behind him.

Julia undressed quickly.

She fell into bed.

Six hours later, at ten o'clock in the morning, she awoke with a start. Someone was knocking.

"Yes?"

"A package for you."

She drew the bed clothes around her. "Just set it inside the door."

The sentry complied.

Julia got up. She felt completely refreshed. She showered.

Opening the package, she was delighted with the clothing the colonel's secretary had selected.

She dressed and combed her hair.

When she tried to leave the hotel room, the sentry barred her way.

"What about breakfast?"

"Order whatever you want from room service," the man told her.

Julia closed the door. I should show him — ! she thought.

But then: Where could I go if I did go out? Suppose they

come for me and I'm gone?

She phoned for breakfast.

The guard stood by while it was brought in. To keep me, she thought, from talking to the waiter.

By noon she still had received no word from the government. She was growing annoyed.

It was after two o'clock when the colonel — the same one who had met them at the airport last night — came for her. "Sorry to keep you so long," he said. "They're ready to see you now."

"I'm ready."

"We're going over to the Pentagon."

"Let's go."

They stopped to pick up Walt.

He had gotten a razor from somewhere; the stubble on his face was gone. His skin was smooth and boyish. He was dressed in a single breasted, brown suit. His white shirt was open at the neck.

Julia's heart caught in her throat with pride when she saw him. She blushed.

"He's been pacing the floor for the last hour," the guard said.

"We're going to talk to some government official," Julia said. She smiled up at him. "How do you feel, Walt?"

"I'm fine. Fine. Nervous. But I feel fine."

"They're waiting," the colonel said. "We better hurry."

Julia took Walt's hand. "It's all right. You don't need to be afraid."

"I'm not afraid," he said.

The same olive drab car was waiting for them outside the hotel. They got in — the colonel in front with the driver, Walt and Julia in back.

The car moved into Washington traffic.

Bleak, harsh winter lay over the town; the very air seemed weary and exhausted. Julia stared out the window at the passing buildings.

The invasion, she thought. Flying saucers settling down upon such a commonplace, solid scene as this. Terrified faces in the streets. Crys. The whine of a police car. An air raid warning, wailing like a lost night express. Brick and cement buckling and exploding. Walls crashing. Smoke billowing up. The helpless, ironic chuckle of a machine gun seeking a target. The drone of a plane. . . .

Suppose the government won't believe our story after all! she thought.

"You're going to help us all you can, aren't you, Walt?" she whispered. Her fingers plucked nervously at her dress.

"This morning, I had a long talk with the man at my door. I'll help you all I can. He'd never even heard of Lyria; he —"

The colonel swiveled his head. "We consulted with the President this morning."

Julia felt herself grow tense. "Yes?"

"He instructed us to have the two of you interviewed by some of the best authorities we could round up on such short notice. You will be required to demonstrate this ability you seem to have to teleport objects."

"I'll do everything I can."

The colonel grunted and turned back to watching the road.

The Tidal Basin lay to one side of the car; the Washington Channel to the other. Off the highway, the rotunda dome of the white marble Jefferson Memorial glistened in the weak sunlight; the cherry trees around it were naked with winter.

Julia listened to her own breathing; she forced herself to relax. I've got to convince them, she thought.

In spite of her superiority, she felt like a little girl venturing into a big, unfamiliar world.

Shortly, the car drew up at the huge Pentagon building.

Inside it, army men — officers and enlisted men — were scurrying about, up and down ramps, in and out of the endless maze of corridors. There was a brisk hum of voices; it was like a giant bee hive. The high heeled shoes of female personnel chattered efficiently from room to room.

"Stay close," the colonel said. "It's easy to get lost."

* * * *

All the noises of the building were swallowed up when the colonel closed the office door on the third floor. The elderly female receptionist at the desk looked up.

"They're waiting, Colonel Robertson. Go right in."

"Right through here," the colonel said.

Walt and Julia followed.

He opened the door, and they issued into the conference room. Talking broke off; faces swung to confront them.

"Gentlemen," the colonel said, "this is the girl, and this — this is the man from the space station."

The audience around the table rustled.

"You'll sit right here," the colonel told them. He helped Julia to her chair. When they were both seated, the colonel withdrew.

Chairs scraped and squeaked.

One of the men across from Julia cleared his throat. He was in civilian clothes. He was slightly stooped and partly bald. He wiped his glasses nervously. "We would like a demonstration of your — your, um, um unusual propensities." He adjusted his glasses.

The glasses disengaged themselves from his ears and floated toward Julia. Julia stood up and walked through the table toward them.

She reached out. Both she and the glasses vanished.

One of the general officers made a check mark on his note book. "I'd say our report is substantially correct."

The other civilian in the room, a youngish blonde woman, lit another cigarette." The ash tray before her was overflowing. Her fingers were nicotine stained. "Very extraordinary."

Julia materialized back in her chair. She replaced the glasses.

The conferees began to whisper softly.

The blonde nodded her head. She turned to Julia. "About this space station —"

"This is Doctor Helen Norvel," one of the general officers told Julia.

Dr. Norvel ignored him. "Is there some way we could detect it?"

"I'd like to try to explain the nature of the distortion field surrounding it to a physicist."

"Dr. Norvel," someone said, "is one of our better experimental physicists."

"Oh?"

"Gentlemen," Dr. Norvel said, "let me talk to her in the next room while you question this man."

The bald civilian said, "Go right ahead, Doctor."

The doctor stood up. Lighting another cigarette, she said, "We'll go right in there, if you don't mind."

Julia got to her feet.

When they had gone, a lieutenant sitting beside the civilian looked up from a sheaf of papers in front of him. "Walt Johnson, isn't it?"

Walt gulped. He felt clammy and frightened.

"I'm supposed to interrogate you — ask you some questions."

"All, all right," Walt said nervously.

"Now, Mr. Johnson, if you'll just tell us — take it slowly; take your time — about life on this space station. Any details you can remember will prove helpful. Describe your quarters, the nature of the aliens — anything at all."

Walt twisted in the seat. He looked around at the waiting faces. A general lit a cigarette. The heating system hummed softly.

Walt began to talk.

From time to time, someone interrupted him with a question.

It seemed to go on forever.

"About this focus rod?"

"It sends out a, a radiation. Something. I don't understand too well. It's lethal."

"What is the radius of destruction?"

"I don't know; I don't remember."

Pens scribbled.

"Please continue," the lieutenant said.

Walt's throat grew dry as he talked. Someone got him a drink of water.

"Could you estimate the number of mutants in this other compartment?"

"I couldn't say. I couldn't swear that there is another compartment."

"A hundred? Five hundred?"

"I couldn't say."

"I see."

"About," a general asked, "how much of the total area of the ship would you say your compartment occupied?"

On and on.

"Let's go over the description of that machine again. Did you ever see this Fierut disassemble any part of it?"

Walt was limp and exhausted. His mind was dulled by the effort of concentrating continuously. "Yes." "No." "To understand that. . . ." "I don't know." "No, no more than that. . . . Please. I'm getting confused."

"You've been very helpful, Mr. Johnson," the lieutenant said. "Gentlemen, I'm afraid he's getting a little tired. Shall we postpone further questioning?"

"I believe we better. Would you call in Dr. Norvel, please."

Walt slumped down in his seat.

The conferees whispered among themselves and compared notes. Julia and the doctor came back.

"It took longer than I thought," Dr. Norvel said. "I had to teach her quite a bit of math."

"What's your opinion?" the bald civilian asked.

"I believe her, gentlemen. She has just shown me how to build some electronic equipment. I'll have a picture of that space station for you within two weeks."

"That will be all, then, for right now," the civilian said. He nodded at Walt and Julia. "The colonel is waiting to take you back to your hotel."

"You're not to talk to anyone about this," one of the generals said.

Thursday. They came for Walt and Julia at nine o'clock. The hotel was aswarm with the military.

"Security measures," the colonel explained as they waited for the elevator. "If any information about this leaks out, the whole country will be thrown into a panic."

Julia nodded.

"We've evacuated the civilians to another hotel," the colonel said.

Two guards with rifles stood at the street doorway.

"It's going to be a hard day for you both," the colonel said once they were in the car. "You're scheduled to meet representatives of some foreign countries at ten o'clock. And after that, we'll spend the rest of the day picking both your brains as clean as we know how."

"That's the way it's got to be," Julia said. "I understand."

It was after midnight when she returned to her hotel. Surprisingly, she was able to sleep until dawn. She arose and showered in the first sunlight and dressed and ordered breakfast. The sergeant on duty at the desk downstairs went out himself to get it for her.

At nine (this was Friday morning) she and Walt were back in the Pentagon. Walt's face was puffy, his eyes were red. "I'm tired," he murmured as an officer hurried him toward a meeting with the Ordnance Section. For a moment Julia considered restoring his mutant bridge. But she was not completely certain that she could trust him; even the tiniest doubt was an excuse not to — since there was no overwhelming advantage to be gained from having two mutants instead of one in the Pentagon.

A few minutes later, Julia was ushered into the office of one of the very high ranking general officers. He rose to greet her, and then returned to his desk. Julia sat down across from him and he pushed stacks of reports to one side until he located his cigarette box.

Julia took a cigarette.

"Julia? I may call you that?"

"Please do."

He bent across the desk to light her cigarette. He pushed an ash tray toward her.

"I expect you'd like to know what we've done so far?"

"Very much."

"I'm preparing a report for the President. I hope to have it for him by noon." He glanced at his watch. "I want to verify with you everything that goes into it."

The smoke made Julia dizzy. She cleared her brain. It was a relief to hear someone else talking for a change.

". . . we're preparing an atomic rocket to intercept their space station," he said. "I understand from this report that your mutant powers aren't infinite. It says in here somewhere that it would be impossible to stop by, by teleportation you call it, don't you? an object as large as a rocket?"

"It's mostly a question of inertia. There's a mass-speed-time ratio involved. The greater the first two, the more time required to divert the missile from its path. The mass-speed must be sufficient to create a greater diversion period than exists between the time of detection and the time of impact."

"You would say that the rocket could get through?"

"If the same rule holds for the aliens as for us, I don't think they would have time to teleport it away."

"That's what I wanted."

"Just a minute, though. How long will it take you to complete it?"

"Give us another week," the general said. "That's one of the things I wanted to see you about. It will take Doctor Norvel longer than that to plot the orbit of the station. I want you to plot that orbit for us —"

"I'm sorry, General. This is in your reports somewhere, too. I can't. Not until Doctor Norvel can locate it. It's too far out for me to locate. I'd have to have an, an anchor on that end — something I could contact — before I could center on it. And I don't have. I can't even feel it, if you see what I mean. There's, nothing to get ahold of. If I could . . . I could just teleport an atom bomb there, and we wouldn't need to worry with the rocket at all." She snubbed out her cigarette.

"Couldn't you get a fix on this frequency that controls your mutant powers and locate the space station that way?"

"Neither Dr. Norvel nor I could detect it with the available equipment: we tried. There's no way of knowing what equipment's required. It's probable the frequency is displaced from normal space; if it is, we can't even tell the increment of displacement. It's just a hopeless task."

"Well, it will take us two weeks or more, then. . . ." He crossed out something on the paper before him.

"Suppose they attack before that?"

"I'm coming to that possibility. . . . I see you say here that mutants can be destroyed by bomb concussions because they can't displace sufficiently far without teleporting. What do you mean there?"

"It's complicated. If the bomb has too much inertia to be teleported off target, they have to remove themselves from the blast area. And they can't remove themselves far enough — not in space, but in relation to space; so they'd have to teleport, and that would be fatal."

"Ummm. Bullets?"

"They could displace themselves far enough to avoid a bullet."

The general wrote something down. "How large an explosion would suffice?"

"I believe Dr. Norvel has those figures. I didn't stay long enough to see the results of her computations. She figured it out. They rushed me off somewhere else."

"I'll have to ask her. . . . Now. I'm counting on there being five hundred saucer ships in the first wave. With luck, our Air Force will get a few of them. You say — ah, yes, right here: 'If hit in the air, the pilots cannot displace out of the ship because they would be killed by the fall to Earth.' That's correct, isn't it?"

Julia nodded. "Yes."

"But I expect we'll have to destroy the majority of them after they land; luck only goes so far."

"If they scatter all over the planet?" Julia asked.

"We have bombers alerted."

"Suppose they land in a city? You'd have to bomb immediately. You'd have to destroy the whole area before they could escape. You wouldn't have any time to evacuate the population. But even so, they could destroy the bomber crews with their focus rods before the planes were over the target —"

"Automatic bombers," the general said. "I hope we've got enough of them. As for the populations, I hope they don't land in our cities." He puckered his lips. "I've alerted all our ground forces. We'll have our whole supply of atomic artillery available. Whenever we discover a focus rod in operation, we intend to hit the center of the area of destruction with everything we've got."

"What do you honestly think?" Julia asked.

He shuffled papers, thinking. He looked up from the report. ". . . it will take us over a week to get even partially ready. If they strike before that, we'll be able to kill some of them. If they give us a week, we might even hope to kill half of them — half of the first wave — before we're destroyed. . . . I was hoping you might offer us an alternative, or a supplement; or something."

Julia took another cigarette. She fumbled in her handbag for a match. She lit the cigarette. "No," she said.

"I rather thought not," he said. "I expected you'd have already told us."

"I've thought about it every way I know how. . . . I thought about displacing all of them when they land; keeping them displaced, where they couldn't reach us. . . . But there'll be too many of them. I might be able to hold one mutant in displacement, even if he resisted me. I know more than he does. But five hundred?" She shook her head.

"Could we build a machine to do that job?"

"You'd have the rocket done much sooner."

". . . I expect that's right. I hope they just give us time."

"If I think of anything else —"

"Oh, I wanted to mention that," the general said. "I want to give you a phone number. You can reach me any time, day or night, through it." He wrote it on a piece of paper.

Julia memorized it at a glance.

The general made a few more notes. He glanced at his watch again. "I guess that's the size of it, Julia."

In the space station, the aliens were readying for the invasion.

Lycan had just finished issuing clothing to the mutants in the larger compartment. Once dressed, they were indistinguishable from earthlings. And more important, when the larger transmitter was eventually cut off, Forential's mutants would easily mistake them for earthlings.

Forential had finished assigning sectors of Earth to his own charges. Each was to cover a given area. They were told that the war on the planet was nearing its conclusion; destruction was everywhere. There would be no opposition to bother them. (In reality, Lycan's mutants, the first wave, having taken care of that.) They could clean up their assigned sectors slowly, thoroughly, methodically. Forential instructed them in all the details of detecting and tracking down earthlings. A month after their arrival, they would be, Forential said, the only survivors.

★★It is,★★ the Elder commented covetously, ★★one of the prettiest little planets I've ever seen. We will be well rewarded for our work.★★

XI

Julia awakened with a start very early Saturday morning. It was not yet three o'clock. Washington lay silent beyond her window. The dark, chill air of the room was motionless.

I forgot to seal Walt's mind off from Calvin's! she thought in blind terror.

She fumbled her bed clothes off and swung her feet to the carpet.

But once she was standing, the effects of the nightmare began to dissipate. She was surprised to find herself trembling. She laughed nervously. She had dreamed that Walt was crossing the carpet toward her bed, walking in silent invisibility. He had raised a knife to plunge it into her heart — had raised a great rock to smash her skull — had aimed a pistol at her brain — while she lay in chill terror, waiting, helpless.

The cold made goose pimples on her naked skin. But her own laugh reassured her.

A second of concentration and blood flowed skin-ward, warming her.

She found the light switch.

When the light came on, she heard the guard outside the door shuffle restlessly.

She began to dress. She needed no more sleep. She was anxious to get back on the job — trying to stop the invasion; although now, in spite of her mutant powers, now that the course of action was outlined, she seemed more in the way than of assistance.

Now why, she thought, would it suddenly seem so important that I should seal off Walt's mind? Yesterday, when he was so tired, I almost gave him back his mutant powers. I do trust him, don't I? Of course. After all the help he's given us, I know — there's not the tiniest doubt, really — that he's completely on our side.

Now why — ?

Seal . . . off . . . mind. . . .

She tried to ignore the thought. It isn't that important, she argued with herself.

Seal . . . off . . . mind. . . .

Whoa! she thought. Seal off *minds!*

Minds.

Harmonics . . . powerful signal . . . transmit . . . blanket. . . .

Pulling her blouse hastily over her head, she realized that it might be remotely possible!

As she reached for the phone, she tried to see the mathematics involved. I'll have to consult Dr. Norvel, she thought.

She dialed. Her hand began to tremble with eagerness.

The phone rang in her ear. Once. Twice. Three times.

"Hello?"

"Hello, this is Julia. Let me speak to the general. Hurry!"

Whoever was on the other end of the line moved quickly. Julia could hear a phone ringing in the receiver.

"Yes?" the general said, sleepy-voiced.

"Julia, General."

"Yes?"

"I *think* I've got something for you."

"Yes?"

"If we can transmit a powerful enough signal, we might be able to create harmonics that would interfere throughout the possible displacement area. Interfere with the frequency that closes our bridges, I mean. It's the same principle as concussion affecting the displacement area."

"Wait a minute. Okay, go on. I'm recording this, now."

"If our television and radio transmitters will handle the signal, we can blanket the whole planet with interference. Any mutant that hits it will automatically be deprived of his mutant powers."

"What . . . ?"

"Look. We can make the whole first wave human normals. The Army can round them up and keep them unconscious while we adjust our interference to meet the second wave."

"I see, vaguely. What do you need?"

"Dr. Norvel."

"I'll phone her."

"A laboratory. An electronics laboratory."

"I'll get it."

"Enough time."

"All I can do on that score is hurry as fast as I can. As soon as I get your laboratory, I'll send a car around for you."

"Right."

"I've got calls to make, then. You give me the details later."

"Goodby."

Julia hung up.

She felt elation. She went to the window and breathed deeply. The air was exciting.

Two hours later, she was in a staff car speeding toward an experimental laboratory on the outskirts of town.

She was hustled inside the building by a sergeant and a colonel; gray, cloudy dawn hovered in the east.

Dr. Norvel was already waiting.

"Let's go to work," the doctor said.

"Right."

"What do you propose? The general said something about interfering with the frequency controlling your mind. How? We can't even detect it."

"We don't need to. We generate a signal, vary the frequency until I lose my mutant powers — and that's it! We generate as strong a signal as we can. Then we have every transmitter in the country put on a direct line to us. When the radar spots the first saucer, we let go with every kilowatt of power we've got."

"Good, good, good," Dr. Norvel said excitedly. "See if you can find some good coffee, you there, with the bird on your shoulder."

The colonel said, "Yes, ma'am."

"I'll try to get some electronics men in to help," Dr. Norvel said. "We may need plenty of help."

"Is there a technical library around?" Julia asked. "I better read up on electronics."

"There's one in there," the puzzled night watchman said.

"I want you to get me somebody from the Army that can get me equipment, and fast," Dr. Norvel told the sergeant. He was standing helplessly by the door.

"I —"

"Hurry up, damn it!"

The sergeant shrugged in resignation. "All right, but they won't like it. I'm the one you should have sent for the coffee."

After, the sergeant was gone, the colonel came back.

By noon, the laboratory was alive with activity.

By six o'clock, the signal generator was beginning to grow.

Julia supervised the crew laying cable. The cable would be connected to the nearest radio transmitter.

"Your transmitter will handle our signal?" Julia asked.

"You give it to us, and we'll tell you."

A general interrupted Julia. "I'm from General Tibbets. How's it going?"

"Can't tell."

"We're trying to scatter paratroops — detachments of them. All over. How long do we have?"

"It's up to *them*," Julia said. "I don't know when we'll be finished here."

"Our men should be stationed by morning."

"I hope we're through that early."

"You disarm these damned mutants, and we'll capture them."

"Hope to."

In the yard, a crew was unloading a new power supply.

"Knock a hole in the east wall and take it inside!" a harried officer bawled hoarsely.

"Some ass of a newspaper man did a report on unusual activity in the Pentagon and around Washington," Dr. Norvel said. "He hinted it had something to do with the flying saucer reports of twenty some years ago."

"How in hell did it leak?"

". . . the Pentagon's issuing a denial."

By midnight, Julia was superintending the construction of a second signal generator. Work on the first one was temporarily stalled; the technicians were waiting for a special transformer.

Dr. Norvel was waving an inked-in schematic diagram before the face of a gray haired man in an apron. "No, no, no," she said. "It's got to be this way to set up the right harmonics."

A major came up and tugged apologetically at Julia's arm. "Are you in charge here?"

"I'm sure I don't know."

"Well, if you are — please, Miss, my men have to rest. Can I let them go now?"

"We're not quiting 'til we finish — I'm sure of that."

The major went away, looking for someone else in authority.

Walt, his mutant bridge restored, was inspecting the second signal generator with interest. With it, the technicians would determine the signal that interfered with his frequency. They would set it to throb out that signal.

One section of the transmitter cable ran to each signal generator. A sergeant had just finished installing a switch that would control the signal being fed into the output line. After the first mutant wave had been captured, the switch would be thrown to the left. The signal covering Walt's powers would then be transmitted to the same network of radio and television stations that had carried the one covering Julia's; and the second wave would be reduced to earth normal.

It was dawn before the first signal generator began operation. It was Sunday.

Julia sat at a desk, sipping coffee, holding a book suspended in front of her, six inches from the desk top. The last twenty-four hours had left a strain on her face. When the book fell, her mutant powers would be gone.

Smoking cigarette after cigarette, Dr. Norvel watched. After nearly fifteen minutes, she pleaded, "Drop, damn you, *drop!*"

Work on the second generator continued. It was at least half a day away from completion. There was a continual mutter of conversation about it in the background.

An hour later, sweat covered Julia's face. The book was still suspended.

"Put in the next frequency range unit," Dr. Norvel said wearily.

A general bustled in. "General Tibbets wants to know how we're doing here."

Silence greeted him.

"The paratroopers are ready," the general said defensively.

Lycan bustled about, making last minute preparations in the larger compartment. His faceted eyes gleamed with excitement. Now and then he spoke to a mutant.

"You ready, Fred?"

"Yes, Lycan. I'm nervous, but I'm ready."

"It's natural," Lycan reassured.

The mutants shuffled their feet and cleared their throats and wiped their palms. They smiled uneasily.

"Form a line!" the Elder called. "We're ready to load you."

The mutants complied. They spoke in hushed undertones. Their focus rods, like tall staffs, bristled unevenly above their heads.

Lycan led them up the ladder to the second level. Led them down the long corridor. Led them past gleaming, whirring machinery.

In the huge, open launching area, the other aliens made last minute adjustments on the saucer ships.

The Elder sent the first group forward. They boarded their ships. The aliens withdrew.

A section of the wall unfolded. Air hissed away, expelling the saucer ships out into space. The mutants worked their simple controls. The saucer ships floated together as if for protection. On signal, they plunged earthward.

The section of the wall folded back. Air entered. The aliens rushed out and unloaded more saucer ships from the storage compartments.

Mutants entered and boarded. The aliens withdrew. The wall unfolded. A second group of saucer ships plunged earthward. The wall folded back. It was as if the space station had opened its mouth; as if the mouth had breathed flying saucers.

Down they came.

Early Sunday sunlight burst across the eastern part of the North American continent.

Nearly a thousand saucers, in five compact groups, one group for each continent, slipped one after another into the atmosphere.

There was no opposition. No planes rose to challenge them. They braked and flattened and skimmed toward their assigned landing sites.

And they touched down: in the hearts of industrial cities; in farm communities; at military installations. They streaked up from the horizon; they hovered; they settled gently to earth.

A few surprised early risers saw them flashing across the sky; saw them land; saw the mutants, armed with focus rods, step out and adjust themselves to the openness all around them. Hate was stamped plainly on the mutants' faces. They took their time, adjusting their focus rods for death and destruction. The few earthlings who saw them waited or fled or advanced with curiosity.

At the Infantry School at Ft. Benning, Georgia, a saucer landed in the third cortile. The three jump towers to the left were like bony fingers pointing accusingly at the sky.

The troops, alerted, uncertain as to what they were waiting for, were lounging in the barracks. Their orders had been changed several times in the last few days. An orderly coming from "C" Company rec hall saw the saucer first. He watched the female mutant get out, look around, shudder and shrink upon herself beneath the horrible, distant sky.

He went to report it to the O.D.

The female began to adjust her focus rod.

At the airport across the Chattahoochee River in Alabama, five battalions of paratroops were waiting assignment. They had been briefed on their jobs less than twelve hours ago. Cargo planes warmed up off the runways, poised for service.

The hastily organized message center was the focus of frantic activity. A teletype chattered. Telephones from radar stations rang and were answered. A harried clerk slipped a scribbled slip to a major waiting beside the desk. He read it, whistled, and trotted toward the main body of troops.

"There's one over in the third cortile."

A nervous captain stood up and field-stripped his cigarette. "Want me to jump — or take a truck?"

"Jump," the major said. "There's planes."

"Yes, sir."

"Load the third platoon," the captain called.

A transport, under instruction from a colonel, wheeled onto the runway.

The colonel came running up. "Load that platoon for Birmingham, Captain," he ordered. "Radar traced one down there."

"There's one in the third cortile on the Main Post," the major said.

"Get it with the next plane," the colonel said.

The major trotted off to get a plane.

The captain told a lieutenant: "Take the fourth platoon, Hawkins."

The lieutenant saluted self-consciously. He crossed to his assignment and began to check his men's equipment. The men pulled nervously at their parachute harnesses and puffed at their cigarettes. "Don't forget to hook up in the plane."

Several men were waving out the next transport. It lumbered forward as the other one cleared the field and circled west toward Birmingham.

"I'd feel better with a rifle," one of the troops told the lieutenant.

"What the hell," one of the other men said, "You'd have to

clean it when you got back!"

"Let's go!" the lieutenant said.

The platoon moved into the waiting transport.

A medical aide trailed up at the rear, carrying his hypodermic kit. Once the platoon overcame the mutant, he would inject enough morphine to knock the mutant out for at least twenty-four hours.

The female in the third cortile saw the lumbering transport, saw the silken blossoms swaying down from it. It amused her to wait. She was in no hurry. She was going to take it slowly at first: savoring the first few: before killing became a mere impersonal, mechanical operation.

The soldiers were unarmed. They landed, divested themselves of their chutes, trotted toward an assembly area designated by the lieutenant. When they were grouped, they started to close in on her — advancing nervously.

She lifted the focus rod. So this was the best they could send against her! She concentrated. She would turn them into flaming torches. Then she would demolish all the buildings within range. But first the screaming human torches. . . .

Nothing happened. The focus rod was as useless as wood.

Her mind was cramped. It was no longer as alert as it had been in the space station. She was now adjusted to the openness around her. She realized something was badly wrong.

The soldiers, smiling now, were almost upon her.

She dropped the focus rod and started to run.

In Washington, Walt and Julia waited by the signal generator that was in operation, broadcasting its interference across the whole planet. Julia, bereft of her mutant powers, sat limply in a folding chair; her body was a stupor of exhaustion; she watched the activity around her with listless, heavy-lidded eyes.

General Tibbets paced nervously before the second generator.

Dr. Norvel hovered at the control panel.

"It's finished," a technician said, straightening stiffly from the electrical wiring at the rear of the panel.

The general stopped pacing. "Walt! Are you ready?"

"Okay," Dr. Norvel said. "Turn it on."

"I'm ready," Walt said.

A power supply moaned.

"Here we go, Walt."

A technician ran a hand through his hair. "Keep your fingers crossed."

Walt, seated beside Julia, concentrated on the book. It floated above the desk.

Dr. Norvel moved the dial. Her face was pale and drawn.

The general coughed nervously.

The control light of the generator winked out.

Everyone held his breath.

The air was filled with the sharp, acrid odor of burning wiring.

"Unplug it!" Dr. Norvel cried.

A technician cut off the power.

"Oh, damn, damn, damn," Dr. Norvel said tonelessly.

The generator still smoked. A technician was trying to see into the wiring behind the panel. "Something shorted," he said unnecessarily, "It's a mess."

"We've got to get it fixed," Julia said dully.

Dr. Norvel collapsed, crying quietly. "It's too late; it's too late; it's too late."

"We worked too fast —"

Walt stood up. The book fell with a sharp, explosive sound now that he had stopped concentrating on it. "We'll have to find my frequency on the other generator."

"Not until we get all the first wave of mutants under control," Julia said. "We can't shut off their interference before."

"Suppose it takes as long on your frequency as it did on Julia's?" Dr. Norvel said. ". . . I don't think we've got that kind of time. As soon as they realize something's wrong. . . ."

"What else can we do?" Walt asked.

Nobody answered.

Dr. Norvel rummaged nervously through her smock. "Anybody got a cigarette?"

The general fumbled in his uniform. ". . . I'm out . . . Colonel?"

"I'll send out for some, sir."

"Try in my handbag," Julia said. "I think there's some there."

The general went to the handbag. He opened it. He removed the birth certificates and found the cigarettes.

Dr. Norvel took one from him and lit it. "Thanks."

"What's these?" the general asked.

"Birth certificates," Julia said.

"Uh — ?"

"Of some of the mutants," Julia said. "I kept them, kept them to establish paternity. When they were all captured."

The general tossed them on the table. "It doesn't look like we'll need them. . . . Well, let's get that second machine going."

Technicians were already stripping out burned wiring. One of them was scribbling a list of replacement parts on a loose sheet of paper.

"I better see how many we've captured, so far," the general said. "How long it will take to get them all."

The colonel stood respectfully aside, and the general walked heavily to the office.

The laboratory was silent. After they heard him speak into the telephone, the technicians resumed conversation, hushed and hopeful, and nervous.

The general listened to the staff report from the Pentagon.

The overall situation was confused. The Army had no idea of how many mutants were still at large. Some had gone into hiding, and dressed as earthlings, they were impossible to identify by appearance.

A group of civilians had reported one mutant in custody. They had been told to knock him unconscious and keep him unconscious until further word.

Since all radio and television transmitters were in use, it was impossible to solicit aid from the great body of civilians — most of whom, indeed, knew nothing as yet of the invasion; most of whom were jamming switchboards with angry calls aimed at determining why their television sets weren't working. The official explanation, issued by the stations themselves, was sunspots.

The general listened quietly.

"Break it to the press," he said at last. "Ask that all civilians cooperate."

The Pentagon resumed the report.

It was estimated that more than eight hundred saucers had already landed across the planet. There was only a little information so far from foreign countries, all of whom had been alerted. Russia had reported nineteen mutants captured. England reported two. France —

"Thanks," the general said.

The Elder detected the interference when a control needle on the frequency transmitter began to jump erratically. Instantly he checked the displacement coupling. There was nothing wrong with it. The frequency was being properly transmitted.

He was petrified with terror. His eyes glazed. His tentacles hung limp. Breath gurgled in his body; bubbled and rattled and rasped.

Then, leadenly, he moved one tentacle.

★★Conference!★★ he shrieked to his colleagues. ★★Conference,★★ he sobbed brokenly.

Circuits opened up; the Elder gave them his knowledge.

They had no difficulty in deducing the general picture of what was happening on Earth.

★Walt failed,★★ they accused Forential.

★★Save us, Elder! Save us!★★

There was a hysterical babble of thought throughout the space station.

Forential raced down the ladder like a tumbling spider. He threw himself along the second level corridor. He stopped, gasping, before the frequency transmitter governing his charges.

It still functioned perfectly.

The other aliens fled aimlessly through corridors, huddled in dark corners; they whimpered and moaned and waved their tentacles in terror.

Make peace! one of them screamed shrilly.

Surrender!

They'll kill us anyway! Don't be a fool!

No, no, no!

Lycan embraced the Elder for protection. Trembling, he looked up into the Elder's contorted face. They both sobbed dryly.

Forential could not think. He was paralyzed.

It was almost half an hour before they quieted.

My mutants aren't jammed, Forential told them for the dozenth time. **Maybe there's still hope.**

**Send them all down; send them all — **

No! Wait! Fierut interrupted sharply. **Wait! Reason! Suppose there is interference on Forential's frequency. Suppose it just isn't strong enough for us to detect it. Suppose they're throwing most of their power into interfering with Lycan's transmitter. Suppose there is only local interference with Forential's. We've got to take that into account.**

Great hopeless whimpers echoed in their minds.

Wait, now, wait! Fierut commanded. **We must assume it's true. But if we throw all available power into Forential's transmitter, maybe we can breach that purely local interference.**

Yes? Yes? Yes?

**Lycan: cut off your transmitter. Channel every unit of power to Forential — **

**Madness — **

Suicide — !

They could change over — !

There was a rising babble of protest.

Earth can't tell it's off! Fierut thought. **They must be using the two mutants down there for negative tests. They couldn't possibly have detection equipment for a displaced field.**

It's, it's our only hope the Elder whispered.

Fierut scuttled out of his compartment and down the ramp to the instrument room. He began to analyze and test and measure the beams of interference pouring from Earth. He used a synchronized model of the planet to pin-point originating sites. He traced the beams back, Earth transmitter by Earth transmitter, back to the originating site of least distortion and sharpest harmonics. ★★There!★★ he cried. ★★I have located their signal generator!★★

★★All the power is now on Forential's transmitter,★★ Lycan thought. ★★My transmitter is off.★★

★★Send five of your charges down to destroy the signal generator!★★ the Elder ordered Forential. ★★Hold the rest in reserve — in case of more trouble — ★★

Forential dropped down the ladder to the rim level. He was chattering in nervous excitement.

Gasping painfully he selected five of his best mutants.

"Come!" he cried. "I will explain as we go. Traitors on Earth. . . . Walt is a traitor. . . . Hurry!"

"I'll come too," Calvin cried eagerly. "I'll come too!"

"You stay here!" Forential ordered.

★★When the installation is destroyed, prepare to switch your transmitter back on again, Lycan,★★ the Elder ordered. ★★If any of your mutants are alive, they can resume destruction.★★

★★If all goes well,★★ Forential thought, ★★we may yet succeed. I will reassign sectors among my remaining charges.★★

Shortly five new saucer ships left the space station.

The five saucers, in V-formation, careened into the atmosphere. They circled the planet, slowing. The leader peered at a floating needle in a spherical container of liquid. The needle vibrated in answer to the beam of interference it was attuned to. The silver tip wobbled back and forth across the target.

The ships leveled out over the Rocky Mountains. Losing altitude, they hurtled on a sloping trajectory toward Washington.

Across the Great Plains. Across the turgid, swollen Mississippi River. Across the Appalachians, worn and old.

They slowed. The controls became more sluggish.

They hovered over Washington. The needle dipped.

Below, white and massive with afternoon sunlight, the Washington Monument, the tallest piece of masonry on the planet, loomed up between The Ellipse and the Tidal Basin, towering 555 feet into the air: standing rooted and solid and defiant.

Walt *felt* them.

"Mutants from my compartment!" he cried.

Instantly all activity in the laboratory ceased. It resumed almost immediately, pointless and frantic, now.

"They've been sent to destroy our signal generator," Dr. Norvel said matter of factly.

Technicians glanced anxiously at the suddenly unsubstantial walls. There was no protection. They were exposed as completely as if they were alone on a flat, barren tennis court of infinite dimensions.

"Cut off the transmitter!" the general ordered. "Find Walt's interference frequency!"

". . . too late," Julia said. "We haven't time."

"We could be lucky!" the general insisted. "Pick a frequency range. Maybe we can hit the right one. Hurry up, for Christ's sake; you, there — !"

"But we can't cut the transmitter off," Dr. Norvel pleaded. "It would release the other mutants. Give them even five minutes. . . .
"

"I can hold them off for awhile," Walt said. "I can shield myself from the radiations of the focus rod. All the mutants have to be able to. I think I can shield the building against them; I think I have the advantage of knowing more than they do. I don't know how long I can hold such an extended shield — Until they come in after me, I guess."

"We'll stop them," the general said. "We'll stop them at the door."

"You can't," Julia said. She was slowly rousing from her stupor. "They can displace."

"I can't hold off five of them long," Walt said. "Not and hold the shield."

"It would be a greater risk, cutting off Julia's frequency, searching for Walt's."

"But Julia could help him then!" the general said.

"No, because then those on *her* frequency would come after

us. There's more of them." Dr. Norvel pressed her forehead wearily.

"We've got to do something."

Walt's voice cut through the confused babble. "I'm trying to reason with them."

". . . he hears their thoughts," Julia whispered.

Activity ceased. Breathing seemed to cease.

Walt stood erect, motionless, grim. His body was taut. His eyes were bright with tension.

Your focus rods can't penetrate! he called to them.

He braced the shielding against another assault. It came and passed. *I can hold the shielding as long as you can!*

We'll come in and kill you. There's five of us.

Friends, it's me. Walt.

Traitor!

No! No, I'm not!

Lies!

Let me — Listen! Forential lied! I, I can prove it! . . . how?

Hell with him!

No, wait! one of the five insisted sharply. Walt didn't catch who. He could hear them in conference.

Then one blocked out the whole conversation and held it blocked out. A moment later, the block faltered and faded. Walt felt uneasy. What had they said? Some trick?

We do know Walt, after all. We may as well listen.

He's a traitor.

Wait. If he has proof — !

He couldn't have: It's Lyrian lies!

Give me a chance! Walt pleaded. I know you all. Give me a chance. What can you lose?

Forential said —

Give me a chance!

Let's hear him.

We owe him that.

Walt was sweating now. His hands were clenched into fists. He was almost certain that the argument was for his benefit: to make their seeming acquiescence less suspicious.

I'm coming out. One of you come to me.

Walt let out his breath. "There's a chance —" He went to the table and scooped up the birth certificates. "I hope one of these fits."

"Walt!" Julia cried. "If it doesn't!"

". . . they were my friends," he said. "I was raised with them. Maybe they'll believe me anyway. Bob and Jim and Dave and Reg and Willy. . . ." Walt shrugged.

He crossed to the doorway. He left the laboratory.

Just outside he waited. One of the five saucer ships approached. He could see Julia's face at the window. It was drawn and pathetic. He wanted to go back and comfort her and tell her everything was going to be all right.

How sweet she was! Now that she was no longer infinitely wise and superior, now that she was dependent and helpless: how sweet she was!

He wanted to protect her. His heart swelled with sadness and with joy.

The saucer ship hovered. He motioned it closer. It drew in toward him like a nervous colt.

He waited.

He motioned it closer.

At last, just in front of him, it jolted down.

Willy got out.

Walt watched as the horror of openness flickered across his face.

You'll get used to it, Walt thought. *You'll like it, when you get used to it.*

Willy clutched the side of the ship for support. *I'm, I'm all right, inside the ship. . . . You come inside.* He clambered back out of sight.

Caution counseled refusal. But Walt approached the entrance. His increased knowledge made him confident. He had learned much — just in the last day. He was more than a match for a single mutant from the space station. If he had known as much last Monday as he knew now, Julia would never have escaped. He entered.

Willy pulled the door closed. He was breathing heavily.

Take off your shoes! Walt commanded. Walt knew Willy was going to try to start the ship, try to move it away so that Walt's shield would no longer cover the laboratory. Once that happened, the mutants on the outside could blast the laboratory in a second.

What?

Slowly, Willy was moving the starting lever by teleportation. Walt located the focus rod.

Take your shoes off!

Suspiciously Willy glanced back mentally at the other saucer ships a short distance behind. Willy hesitated. Then he sat down and removed his shoes. He watched Walt closely. The starting lever continued to inch into position.

Walt knew Willy wouldn't risk a sudden motion.

But Walt was wrong. As he bent down, the lever snapped in place. The saucer shuddered.

And Walt, using the focus rod for power, fuzed the control panel in an instant beyond all use. Before the other mutants could strike, his extended shielding was back around himself and the laboratory.

You're going to listen, Walt told him calmly. *All of you. You're an earthling. Every one of you. You were born here of Earth parents.*

Nonsense!

It's true. You shut up!

Willy waited, uncertain. The others were equally uncertain. They had not been prepared for a failure in their initial plan.

I have proof. Right here. Walt thought all the details to the mutants as rapidly and as sincerely as he could. His face was bloodless. His hand was shaking. The strain of holding the shielding was beginning to tell on him.

Only two birth certificates were left. I've got to make them see that Forential had lied to them! he thought.

The mutants were thinking the situation over in privacy, agreeing on a new course of action.

And there it was!

Wonder of wonders, the last birth certificate was Willy's!

See! See! Walt thought excitedly. *This proves what I was telling you! Look! All of you! They're the same!*

It proves nothing, Bob thought. *It's faked.*

Is that the best you have to offer? one of them sneered.

Let's kill him! Get it over with!

How could I fake it? Walt demanded. He realized now what a pathetic hope it had been. He needed time; given that, the birth certificates would be very helpful in convincing them. But without time, he couldn't give them all the back-*ground they needed. And they weren't going to give him time.

Lyrian traitor!

You can't hold us all off, Walt. We're going to kill you.

Walt saw them — saw them mentally — landing their four ships. In a few minutes they would be upon him.

He began to tremble in impotent rage. He backed toward the door to escape from the confining walls. He tried to make his shielding even stronger against their focus rods.

Julia, waiting in the laboratory, heard her heart beating loudly and rapidly. The one saucer had landed. Walt had boarded it. The four were drifting, waiting. There was a hum from the signal generator behind her. Let him be all right, let him beat them off! she prayed.

What's happening? How can I help?

...Perhaps because her mind was so fatigued that it was almost functioning on the automatic level of sleep, she realized at last why the two compartments in the space station had been kept separate. After the second wave of mutants destroyed the first — under the impression they were the Earth survivors of a war — the aliens would silence the second frequency transmitter. Earth would be populated by less than thirty male mutants. The race of man would not breed back. In a few years, the planet would be ready for its conquerors.

I wish I could tell Walt that, she thought. Maybe it would be of some help to him.

The four saucers landed.

She bent forward tensely.

Has he convinced them? Are they coming out to surrender?

XII

Walt was outside the ship. His feet planted firmly, he waited. The four advancing mutants were not yet adjusted to the space disorientation. Behind them, the tip of the Washington Monument loomed starkly white above the trees.

Walt's anger rose to an even greater fury. He knew how Julia had felt as a child: the hot, impotent flare of rage; the senseless desire to throw something; to smash and destroy something; to disprove helplessness by some savage action.

The mutants were closer; terror was dying out of their eyes. Their lips were relaxing. Their bodies were loosening to their wills.

We're going to kill you, Walt: with our hands.

Lyrian traitor.

Walt was breathing in shallow gasps. They would rush him in a minute. Willy, out of the saucer ship now, crouched only yards away, ready to spring. He feinted, and Walt flinched instinctively.

You can't displace from five of us!

Not and hold the shielding, traitor!

General Tibbets, in the doorway behind Walt, began firing at the mutants with a pistol.

Bob clutched at his chest and staggered. In an instant, the others were displaced and invulnerable.

Bob fell.

Reg went to his wounded companion, held him in displacement, healed him rapidly.

Bob coughed and shook his head and scrambled to his feet. He screamed his hate at the general.

The pistol clicked on an empty chamber.

Walt retreated several steps.

. . . green wartle rivers of Lyria; birdsong, there, in a skybranch, partly pretty orange and soft like fur pictures. . . .

He was in Calvin's mind!

Calvin was sitting in the games space, on the floor, rolling the metal practice ball back and forth before him between his hairy hands. Forential was speaking. The confining walls of the space station were so comfortingly solid. . . .

And Walt had a fix on it! Knew its position, its direction, its speed! He had an anchor!

Where is something? he thought wildly. Quick! A rock! Throw a rock! Something big: to throw: quick! Huge, heavy —

Forgotten, the advancing mutants. With every unit and sub unit and compartment and section of his mind, pouring out every available degree of telepathic power, dropping the shielding, concentrating above everything else, he seized the Washington Monument. It shook; it wobbled unsteadily; it wrenched free.

Calvin, delighted, was helping him.

Walt! he cried. *We'll play games! We'll throw it!*

It was off the ground. It poised uncertainly. It moved upward. Slowly at first, like a rocket: faster and faster, dwindling from Earth, becoming a vanishing pinpoint like a black, daylight star.

Calvin pulled it in with childish joy. *It's* big! he cried proudly.

It was aimed on target.

Calvin was no longer in Walt's mind.

With a last, exhausting burst of thought, he increased its already terrific speed. The laboratory still stood. The mutants had not realized his shielding was down. He restored it, weakened and quivering.

And they were upon him. He fought them off with his fists and elbows. He dared not displace, lest the shielding should crumble entirely. A few minutes more; if I can just gain a few minutes more, he thought.

He was down. He jerked his head out of the way of a foot. He caught a leg and twisted.

Fingers tore at his throat. He caught someone with a savage and satisfying kick.

Out in space, beyond the orbit of the moon, Fierut detected the Washington Monument on his warning device. It was coming too fast to deflect. He tried.

A heartbeat later, it ripped into the steel of the space station. It crumbled and shattered and sprayed marble, and huge fragments erupted from the opposite side. The space station became visible.

There was a great, ragged, tunneling hole from rim to rim. Escaping air spewed wreckage into space. Parts of demolished machinery whirled away. In a yet-sealed compartment, a power system exploded with a great, blinding, soundless flash. Chunks of steel debris, vast shrapnel, blossomed in all directions.

The space station, its orbit altered, twisted away, a gutted, lifeless derelict.

Walt's shielding collapsed. His mutant bridge opened; his mutant powers vanished. He screamed for help.

He saw General Tibbets slam a pistol butt against Willy's suddenly unprotected skull.

Five minutes later, in the laboratory, amid incredible confusion, Julia stood over Walt and dabbed antiseptic on his cut, swollen lip.

Throughout the room there were shouts and laughter and cries of victory. One of the technicians — one who had worked hardest over it — was joyfully smashing the second signal generator.

In the center of the frenzy, Dr. Norvel sat slumped across the desk. She was sound asleep.

Weary and proud, Julia straightened up from Walt.

"I've — we've both — got to get some rest," she said. "There'll be the press, the TV, the radio . . . I can't face them. I'm too tired. . . . I must look like something the cat dragged in. . . . "

Walt, heavy lidded and exhausted, looked up at her. He smiled leadenly. "Look fine, Julia." His voice was thick and indistinct because of the swelling of his tongue.

She sure ran me around, he thought. But she can't now. She's not superior to me any more. I'll be able to hold my own. She's, she's so helpless, so pliant. That's the way I like her. Poor tired girl!

We'll travel, he thought. I want to see all of the planet. All the sights, all the cities. I want to live in the bustle of its life, in the hurry of its crowds. I want to travel and learn all the different smells and experience all the different places, and I want to celebrate its richness and its newness; I want to devour it; I want to —

She'll be there; I want to feel her by my side: sweet Julia, so compliant, waiting my decisions and anticipating my wishes. I want to see her laugh. And I want . . . I want. . . .

I'll have to ask her about things like that.

. . . I'm no longer so innocent, but I'm not yet so wise. I have grown and matured marvelously, and I will further: I know what I want. And she'll be there to, to help me see and do and. . . .

He felt a great warm glow of bursting and bubbling emotions.

"I'm going to sleep twenty-four hours," Julia said. "Just as soon as I can get in bed."

"Better leave before the fourth estate gets here," the general said. "I'll have the staff car drive you back to the hotel."

"Don't tell anybody we're there."

The general nodded. He took Julia's arm. "I'll walk you outside." He sent an orderly for the car.

"When you're rested —" he let Walt and Julia go through the door in front of him — "when you're rested, we'll want to see both of you again. You said something, Julia, about making us all like you were: with all those unusual abilities?"

"Later. Please, later. I'm just too tired to think." She held onto Walt's arm possessively.

But do, she wondered, *do* I remember enough details to enable a surgeon to install a bridge?

A welter of other thoughts and impressions seethed to the surface of her leaden brain: The international situation . . . if nothing changes . . . for the last few years, there is an equilibrium . . . working for genuine peace. . . . War is farther off every year. . . . But to interfere? When people can still be convinced of so many, so many falsehoods? Patterns of hatred (like of superstition), are they (aren't they: who can say? would the bridge not join but divide, upset the equilibrium?) are the patterns of hatred too deep, and too dangerous, and too entrenched in our generation?

She was tired; but out of the exhaustion, the weariness, the fatigue, she suddenly realized with startling clarity, like the chime of a great, flawless bell, ringing hope and promise: That it will come; the next development of man will come, lies waiting in the future (near or far) to be born, to be born: will come. When mankind is ready, it will come: will come.

A wave of exultation filled her. Oh, be ready soon! she cried.

Be ready soon!

"I, I don't think I can, can be of any help on that, General," she said.

"After you get some rest —"

"No," she said. Did she remember enough to guide a surgeon? "No, I'm afraid I've forgotten too thoroughly."

The general helped them into the car.

She snuggled over against Walt. She didn't want to think at all. She dreaded the next few days. She wished they were over.

She pulled Walt's head down and kissed his swollen lips. He tried to draw back in surprise. She held on. The car began to move. He resisted and then relaxed and then cooperated. She was deliriously in love with him.

Drifting to sleep she thought: After next week, we'll be able to get away and go home. We'll settle down right away. We'll buy the Castle Place; he can fix it up and work around the yard in the evenings, and I'll put pink and white curtains in the kitchen. And there's Beck's Hardware Store. I'll have to see about making the down payment on it the first day we get back.

There will be Saturday teas. Walt will look stunningly handsome in a double breasted suit in Church on Sunday. . . .

. . . movies twice a week . . . dancing once a month. . . . I'll let him go moose hunting in Canada every single year if he wants to.

She snuggled closer.

He's so innocent, she thought. He'll have to be educated (not so much as the other mutants, because he's already learned a little): but not more than it is good a husband should be.

My, she thought, feeling his arms around her. My, he has *strong* muscles.

But he won't be any trouble. He'll handle like a lamb. I can manage him.

She smiled and was asleep.

GENERAL MAX SHORTER

I

Miracastle: The initial landing had been made on a flat plateau among steep, foreboding mountains which seemed to float through briefly cleared air. In the distance a sharp rock formation stood revealed like an etching: a castle of iron-gray stone whose form had been carved by alien winds and eroded by acid tears from acid clouds.

Far above was a halo where the sun should be. The sun was an orange star only slightly larger than Sol and as near to Miracastle as Sol to Earth. The orange rays splintered against the fog and gloom was perpetually upon the dark face of existence.

This was the first two-stage planet man had ever attempted to colonize. Miracastle was so far from Earth that the long ships were destroyed twice to reach it.

The technicians came, commanded by General Max Shorter, sixty-three years old. Men wearing the circle whose diameter was etched in ruby steel enclosing a background of gleaming ebon— the emblem was a silver D over a sunburst of hammered gold.

The surface of Miracastle roiled with unfamiliar storms and tornados and hurricanes. Before these, the films of lichen evaporated into dust, and the sparse and stunted vegetation with ochre foliage turned sear and was powdered by the fury in the air.

Earth equipment, alien to the orange sun, hammered into the heart of Miracastle. Night and day it converted the pulverized substance of the planet in the white-hot core of its atomic furnaces.

Acid rivers snapped at the wind and changed to salt deposits and super-heated steam. In the gaseous atmosphere, neutral crystals formed and fell like powdered rain. Miracastle heated and cooled and shivered with the virus of man-made chemical reactions, and the storms screamed and tore at the age-old mountains.

Inside the eternal, self-renewing Richardson domes, the technicians worked and waited and superintended the computers which controlled the processes raging beyond them.

The long ship lifted steadily and majestically through the battering storm and the driving rain of dust and crystals. Out beyond the dense space that surrounds all stars, the long ship probed the ever-shifting currents in the four-dimensional universe. The long ship found a low-density flaw, where space could hardly be said to exist at all. The long ship, described mathematically, was half as long as the continuum—the length being inversely proportional and related only to mass. Time was but a moth's wing between twin cliffs of eternity.

Inside Miracastle's orange sun, at its very core, an atom of hydrogen was destroyed completely; and in the inconceivable distance, an atom of hydrogen appeared. The pulsing, steady-state equation of the universe maintained its knife-edge and inevitable thermo-dynamic balance.

Inside the long ship, a pilot-machine ordered the destruction of a vastly greater collection of matter. The atoms of the ship and the sailors—fixed in relationship, each to each—imploded into nothingness.

And the long ship and the men aboard it were born again at a low-density area a million light years away—halfway to Earth. Born and were destroyed again, in the blink of an eye.

Beyond the ship now lay Sol, pulsing in its own warmth and warming its children embedded in the cold and distant texture of the universe. The sailors were ghosts come home.

Miracastle was alone with her conquerors.

General Max Shorter, a few weeks later, began writing a diary.

"I have been Destroyed thirty-seven times during forty years' service with the long ships," he wrote. He wrote with a pen, using a metal straight edge as a line rule.

"I have served faithfully and I believe as well as any man the

Corps, the planet and mankind. It is perhaps appropriate at this time, as I approach the end of my long service, to record a few observations which have occurred to me during the course of it as well as to record the day-to-day details of my present command."

The general wrote: "A man is given a job to do. And when all is said and done, that is the most important thing in his life: to do his job."

It took perhaps ten seconds for the soft knock to penetrate his concentration. He adjusted himself to the moment and closed the diary softly. He deposited it in the upper right-hand drawer of the writing desk and locked the drawer.

The knock came again.

He arranged his tie.

"Come in," General Shorter said.

The agitation of the man in the doorway was announced by the paleness of his face.

"Come in, David," General Shorter said, rising politely from the writing desk. "Be seated, please."

"General, we've had a . . . a very unfortunate thing happen on the shift."

The general sank back into his chair. Light from the desk lamp framed his expressionless and immobile face, half in light, half in shadow. He fingered the straight-edge on the desk top.

"Sit down, David, and then tell me about it."

Shift-Captain Arnold moved uncertainly.

"Sit down, sit down," General Shorter repeated impatiently.

Captain Arnold seated himself on the edge of the chair.

"One of the men," he said, "just committed suicide. He was in charge of the air changing monitor this shift. He went outside without a suit."

The general blinked as though to remove an irritation from his eye. His hand lay still and hard upon the straight-edge. "What was his name?" he asked in a voice that was vaguely puzzled.

"Schuster. Sergeant Schuster, sir."

"Yes, I remember him," the general said. "He came to us about a week before the lift. I think he was from Colorado. He had very broad shoulders. Short and broad. Neat appearing. Uniform always in good order."

General Shorter ran his thumb and forefinger up the bridge of his nose and then, with a very small sigh, placed his palm over his eyes.

"Draw up the report," he said. "Was there a final message?" The question was uttered without hesitation and was followed by a moment of silence.

"No, sir."

General Shorter's breath was audible.

"Please feel free to smoke, David."

"Thank you, sir, I don't smoke."

"No, of course not. I'd forgotten." General Shorter half turned and placed his hands on the desk. He stood under their pressure. "What would you say to a brandy?"

"I should return to duty, sir."

"A few minutes more," the general said. "The brandy is good." He moved into the shadow and sorted bottles at his tiny cupboard. "Here." He held the glass to the light. Amber liquid flowed softly and the general handed across the half-filled glass. "Sit back," he said. "I'll join you."

Glass in hand, the general stood with his back to the light. He seemed surrounded by cold fire, and the glass sparkled as he lifted it. He sipped. "Try it, it's good."

"It's very good, sir."

For a moment neither spoke. Then the general said, "This isn't my first command, you know. I've seen men die. I've had to take chances with them occasionally. You could say, I suppose, that I ordered some men to their deaths. But still, the men came aboard knowing the risks. In the final sense, they, not I, made the decision. I never sent a—"

The sentence ended as the glass slipped and fell. "I'm sorry," he said, looking down at the sparkling fragments at his feet. The dark liquid—the light gave it a reddish cast—puddled and flowed and its aroma filled the room. "No, no. Let it be, David. I'll get it later."

The general went to the cupboard and poured into a new glass. Again he was light and shadow. The spilled liquid approached the shadow and was devoured in it as though it had never been, but still the aroma stood on the air.

The general said: "Imagine, if you can, David, that Earth were attacked, and the attack destroyed many of the military installations. After you struck back, David, what would you do next?"

"I don't know, sir. I'm not a strategist, I'm afraid."

"What about your cities? The millions of people trapped without supplies—over-running the countryside, looting, plundering in search of food. Carrying pestilence and disease and terror. What would you do, David?"

"Well, I guess I'd try to organize some relief organization or something."

"But David. Anything you diverted to care for these people would limit your ability to fight back, wouldn't it? They would be cluttering up all your transportation, frustrating effective retaliation. Your second move would be to take the bombs which destroy people and not property and . . . use them on your own cities."

Captain Arnold drained his glass. "That would be. . . ." He did not finish.

"Insane, David? No. Rational. Field Commanders must be realists. The job comes first. In this case, the job of defeating the enemy. . . . But what does that have to do with us? Nothing, eh? You're right. Sometimes I like to talk, and I suppose that's one of my privileges. I'm not the idealist I used to be, I guess. I remember when I was your age. I saw things differently than I do now. What used to seem important no longer does. Each stage of development has its unique biological imperatives: a child, a youth, a mature man, look out on the world from a body held in focus to different chemistries. But the job remains." General Shorter held up his glass. "Cheers." He drained it.

Again there was silence.

"David, do you think I'm in much trouble?"

"I'm afraid so, General. The Committee is due to arrive tomorrow."

"I know," the general said. "This suicide isn't going to help us. Tomorrow. Is it that soon? I thought . . . yes, I guess it is tomorrow. . . . Well, we've been here long enough to lose our immunity, so we'll all catch colds."

Captain Arnold stood. "I better get started on my report."

"Poor Sergeant Schuster," General Shorter said. "If anyone's to blame, it must be me."

"He obeyed the orders."

"What did you say?"

"I said he obeyed the orders, sir."

"Of course he obeyed the orders," the general said. "What else could he have done?"

II

The long ship hung in orbit above Miracastle and discharged its passengers. The Scout Ball could handle them: saving energy, which along with time itself, is the ultimate precious commodity of the universe governed by the laws of entropy.

The Scout Ball settled through the dark turbulence undisturbed by the hissing winds. It hovered momentarily in the invisible beacon above the Richardson dome as if both attracted and repelled. It moved horizontally and settled. Suited figures on the surface wrestled with its flexible exit-tube against the storm, fighting to couple it to the lock of the Richardson dome. The exit-tube moved rhythmically until the Scout Ball inched away, drawing it taut. Pumps whirred. The suited figures entered the forward lock of the Scout Ball.

Inside, General Shorter divested himself of the helmet. The suit hung upon him like ancient, wrinkled skin.

He asked, "What time is it?"

Upon being told, he nodded with satisfaction. "Seventeen minutes, total. Good job. Who's in charge?"

"A Mr. Tucker, sir."

"Tucker? Jim Tucker, by any chance?"

"Yes, sir."

General Shorter grunted. "Served with him once. He's probably forgotten. . . . That's all right. I'll keep the suit on."

"I don't think they're expecting you with the surface party, General."

"Probably not or they'd be here. Earth crew?"

"They've been out ten months or so, sir."

"We will have colds, then. Would you take me to Mr. Tucker, please?" To the other suited men he said, "Good, fast job."

General Shorter followed the crewman up the spiral staircase and along the corridor. His hand touched a frictionless wall. "New plastic?"

"This is one of the most recent balls, sir."

"How does it handle?"

"Quite well, sir."

"I miss the Model Ten," he said.

"There's only a few left now, I guess."

"I haven't seen one in years."

The crewman stopped before a numberless panel. He knocked politely. "Mr. Tucker? I have General Shorter here. He came out with the surface party."

Mr. Tucker's voice, the edge of surprise partly lost through the partition, came: "Just a moment."

In silence they waited. General Shorter moved restlessly. Several minutes passed.

The panel opened.

Mr. Tucker was a short, rotund man. His close-cropped hair was graying, although his face was unlined, with the smooth complexion of a child. His irises were gray and gold.

General Shorter stepped forward and introduced himself.

"Come in."

The panel closed.

The two men stood. General Shorter glanced around for a chair.

"Small quarters," Mr. Tucker said. "If you like, sit there. I'll sit on the bed."

They arranged themselves.

"Perhaps you don't remember me?" the general said. "We

served together—what, ten years ago?—for about two weeks on Avalon, I believe it was."

"Yes, I thought that was the case. You have a good memory, General."

"Please," the general said, "just call me Max."

Mr. Tucker considered, without committing himself. He proffered a cigar. The general declined.

Mr. Tucker lighted the cigar carefully, moving the flame several times across the blunt end. He regarded the results without expression. "A cigar should be properly lit, General," he said.

"Yes, yes, I suppose so," the general said. He paused to worry at a wrinkle on his suit. "Good trip out?"

"Routine."

"New ship? I notice this is one of the new Balls."

"Mark Six."

"Ah, those. I've always liked the Mark Six. Solid construction. I've been Destroyed maybe half the time in the Mark Sixes. Each one of the Marks has its own personality—I've always thought so. I don't suppose you remember the old Mark Two? That was a long time ago. I've been around. We got lost in one once. It picked a pseudo-fault line and . . . well, never mind. Earth the same, I guess?"

"Hasn't changed."

"I don't know when I'll get back," the general said. The statement seemed to dangle as though it were an unfinished question.

"The new detectors have put Miracastle on the fringe of things."

"I've followed the work," the general said. "I try to keep up. It involves a new concept of mass variation, doesn't it?"

"It just about makes it uneconomical to colonize a two-stage planet any more. Or to keep one going."

The general's eyelids flickered. His body moved beneath the wrinkled folds of the surface suit. Cigar smoke curled in the still air.

Mr. Tucker said, "You must have been aware that it would not have been a great loss to have evacuated Miracastle."

The general shuffled in silence. "Yes, sir, I knew the background. It's part of my job to know things like that. You'll find, sir, that I have a strong sense of responsibility. If it's part of my job, I'll know about it."

General Max Shorter abruptly stood and for a moment was motionless, a man deformed and diminished in stature by the ill-fitting surface suit. Expressionless, he looked down, without psychological advantage, at the seated civilian holding the partially smoked cigar.

Later the same day, Mr. Tucker and two of the three other members of the Committee donned surface suits and, together with Captain Meford, the cartographer assigned to Miracastle, they boarded the surface scout.

They arranged themselves in the uncomfortable bucket seats and strapped in.

"Little early for an easy ride," Mr. Tucker commented.

"I've been out before," Captain Meford said laconically. It was his usual manner.

"How long do you think it will take us to get there?"

"Between fifteen and twenty minutes, if I don't hit too much cross wind."

Mr. Ryan, one of the other two civilians, commented, "A long time between cigars, eh, Jim?"

The question was out of place and was ignored without hostility.

Mr. Ryan twisted uncomfortably. At length he said, apologetically, "Dirty, filthy business. I wish it were over with."

"So do I," Mr. Tucker said.

Captain Meford activated the ramp and eased the scout out. It was immediately buffeted by the winds.

"Sorry," he said. "It'll take a minute. Hold tight." The scout moved in three dimensions, erratically. "Wow! Let's set it at about twenty-six inches. Sorry. This will slow us down, but it will ease the bumps on down draft. There. That's better. We're okay now, I think. I guess we can settle back."

Thirty-five minutes later, they came to what was left of the alien city.

Back in the Richardson dome, General Shorter had coffee, in his quarters, with the remaining man on the Committee, a Mr. Flison. They were going through the ritual of conversation.

"This is the first time you've been Destroyed then, sir," the general said. "My first time was so long ago I've forgotten what it feels like."

"I was uneasy in advance," Mr. Flison said. "You read various descriptions about the physical sensations. Intellectually, of course, you draw a distinction, but emotionally you know that the only word which applies is death—pure and simple. But there's no sensation. It happens too fast. You don't even notice it."

Politely attentive, the general had leaned forward. "I don't think it could be put better," he contributed. "That's very apt. You don't even notice it."

Mr. Flison's eyes narrowed in speculation. They maintained the general's own in unwavering focus. He did not acknowledge the compliment.

The general's eyes broke to one side. He moved nervously as though physically to dismiss the tactical error of underestimating his opponent.

"Since this is your first planet," the general said, "perhaps you'd like to see something of the operation? Basically, we have nine Richardson Domes here on Miracastle. Two are the living quarters—the other similar to this. Right now domes Seven and Nine are the more important. They contain the air-changing equipment. We are holding tightly to our completion date, and these two—Seven and Nine—will be pulled out in fifteen days. That is to say, they will, barring any serious interruptions in our work. On schedule, I should point out."

The general poured coffee for himself. Mr. Flison politely declined.

"When you've been in the Corps as long as I have," the general resumed, "the schedule becomes a part of you. Everything—" he held his hands before him, fingers spread, palms facing, and drew them together—"converges on that. It's that simple. Other planets are waiting. In a society as complex as ours, a million—

and I mean this literally, sir—a million decisions must be reviewed if the schedule falls behind. Delay of a critical item of equipment can necessitate an unbelievably vast reassignment of personnel and supply patterns. A small cause reverberates throughout the whole fabric of the space technology."

"General Shorter, I think perhaps you're being carried away a little. I'm sure we have adequate procedures to accommodate minor variations in equipment delivery dates. If we don't, the Lord help us: we'd have been dead long ago."

The general was in the process of forming an immediate reply, but he reconsidered. When he reached for the coffee, which by now was cool and bitter, his hand was trembling.

The general licked his lips. "More coffee? No? Well, I didn't intend to get off on this. I really wanted to ask if you'd like to inspect our operations." He glanced at his time piece. "I could show you the present shift operation in Dome Nine."

Mr. Flison rose. "No, General, I don't want to be of any bother. I wouldn't want to interfere with your—work."

III

"City" is not necessarily descriptive: perhaps less so than the application of Euclidean axioms to advanced geometry. Physically, it was this:

1. Three dozen stone arches whose keystones were inverted bowls.
2. A smooth-walled recess in the sheer face of a cliff.
3. A level lip of rock, as precisely flat as though honed, from which the arches seemed to grow.

"Is this all?" Mr. Tucker asked.

"Yes, sir," Captain Meford said.

Mr. Ryan came to the viewing section. "It looks," he said, "as though the cliff were split down to here and then hewn away to leave the structures there and the apron."

"We found no tools, sir. There were no tools here, nor with them."

"Nothing else at all?"

"They left behind some four hundred chips of stone, apparently numbered. We have them in the dome. And there's a two-line inscription on one of the arches. There's nothing else."

High above the men and the ship, the new wind sang in one of the inverted bowls and fluttered lightly over the inscription. It, like the face of the cliff, was oxidizing. Dust filtered down before the recess, alien symbols falling. Life is the recording angel of time. Without life, all ceases.

"Dust," Mr. Tucker said. "Dust . . . dust . . . more dust. Soon the dust will be over everything. When the wind is gone, it will be there to hold our footprints."

Inside the air-conditioned scout, the men shivered.

"How did you come to find them?" Mr. Ryan asked.

"I saw the constructions from the photos, sir. This had been missed by the mapping party. It's easy enough to see why when you see the pictures."

"This the only one?"

"Yes, sir."

"How can you be sure of that, Captain Meford? It's a large planet."

"I had one of the machines scan the remaining maps for geometrical patterns, sir."

"Isn't that done routinely?" Mr. Tucker asked rather sharply.

"Yes, sir. But you see, we've always expected that if we were ever going to encounter intelligent life on a planet, it would be rather widespread. Accordingly—and this is the routine procedure, sir, used, as far as I know, by all contact parties—we ran through a statistically significant sample of the terrain. There was nothing on Miracastle out of the ordinary. There was the typical, low-order vegetable matter, about what we always find. It was a very typical planet, sir."

The third man from the Earth Committee, Mr. Wallace, seldom spoke. When he did, his voice was mild, and there was a sense of child-like wonder in his tone. "The natives?" he asked.

"They . . . had fled when we discovered the city."

"Where did they flee to?" Mr. Wallace asked.

Captain Meford glanced upward. Other eyes followed to end just below the edge of the view screen. Above stood the sheer face of the cliff. Clouds roiled below the summit, obscuring it from view.

"There is a long sloping plateau up there, and a series of natural caves back in the next cliff face," Captain Meford said. This did not seem adequate. He continued: "Most of the air-changing activity starts in the low-lying areas, at first around the dome positions. It advances along an elevation front, gradually drifting up. Little tongues are carried up in advance by the heated currents. The aliens retreated before it. On the plateau you can see the sentries. I guess they posted themselves there, at intervals, between the edge and the new caves, to define the limits of safety. They died there. Six of them. The rest, several hundred, reached the caves. They are dead, too."

"I see," Mr. Wallace said.

"When you first discovered them—?" Mr. Ryan asked after a moment.

Captain Meford hesitated.

Mr. Tucker said: "I believe one of your men killed himself last night—wasn't it? A technician? I was told he felt you could reverse the air-changing equipment in time to save the aliens. I understand that was very much on his mind for the last week or so."

"I'm not too familiar with the man, sir. He was on Captain Arnold's shift, I believe."

"Captain Meford," Mr. Ryan insisted, "when did you say you first discovered the aliens?"

Captain Meford hesitated. The others waited.

"They were then scaling the cliff, sir."

"And General Shorter, was he told of this immediately?" Mr. Ryan asked.

"I don't know when the general was told."

"You discovered them?"

"Yes, sir. I . . . you see, at the time the winds completely prohibited air traffic. As you know, the air scouts are not stable enough until . . . later. Later, I . . . Yes, sir. I discovered them."

"Did you then inform the general?"

"No, sir. I informed the duty officer."

"Did he inform the general?"

"I don't know."

"Why didn't you tell the general?" Mr. Tucker asked.

"I was then in communication with Captain Geiger, and I felt he. . . ." The sentence trailed away.

"Would tell the general?" Mr. Tucker prompted. "Well, did he?"

"I believe he did, sir," Captain Meford said. He let out a long breath.

"May we see the aliens?" Mr. Ryan asked.

"I wouldn't advise it, sir," Captain Meford said. "High flights are still very risky because of the wind velocities."

After the evening meal, General Shorter called Captain Arnold aside. "Mind if I go over to Nine with you?" he asked. "The air around here is—well, the fact of the matter is, I'd like to get away from them for awhile."

"Of course not, sir," Captain Arnold said.

"We'll call it an inspection. Which might be a good idea at that. With these people running around trying to interfere with my schedule. Poking around. Asking questions. Taking men away from their work, basically." He tapped his teeth with his right thumb in reflection. "I'd better check up on all the domes tonight, just to be sure."

"Yes, sir."

"I wouldn't want anything to go wrong because they're here."

In the dressing quarters, they donned surface suits and exited through the locks to Miracastle. In the area immediately beyond the Dome, the solidly positioned connection rails radiated away. The general gestured for the captain to lead.

The wind buffeted them. Inside the surface suits it was quiet.

"David?" the general asked.

"Yes, sir?" Captain Arnold said. He was fastening his safety line in the keyed slot. He fumbled with it for a moment before the wind.

"You on suit communications?"

"Yes, sir." Captain Arnold straightened and moved forward. The general replaced him and dropped his safety line in place with practiced efficiency.

Captain Arnold, surrounded by dust devils, became a distant, indistinct bulk. His motions were ponderous. The general could no longer see his face or his expression.

"I do not entirely understand this, David," the general said conversationally. "The investigation. I thought I had powerful friends in the Corps. Though a man makes enemies." The general lurched awkwardly over the broken surface of Miracastle, drawing the safety line taut. He moved toward the connection rail again. "A general is separated from much of his command. Some of the technical refinements are too involved—and, of course, men hide their feelings." Once again he struggled with the wind, turning slowly at the end of the safety line: held from the devouring anger of the planet only by the slender umbilical cord from the stars. "General Grisley, now. I think he's sixteen star, in headquarters. He was a politician. He came up fast. In fact, he was my adjutant a few years ago. He was always a man to hold a grudge."

Captain Arnold made no reply.

"You know how politics is in the Corps."

Dome Nine rose from the swirling mist before them. The wind seemed to increase in fury. And still, inside the suits, there was the sound only of labored breathing and the general's voice.

"These natives," the general said. "They were very primitive, David." Neither could see the other's face. "I can't think of them as intelligent at all. I feel they were very low on the evolutionary ladder. I wouldn't call it a city, as I've heard it called. Natural formation, more likely. Nature plays strange tricks."

They were at the lock of Dome Nine.

Inside, the general removed his helmet. "David," he said, "I've been meaning to talk to you for some time now. You've got a good career in front of you in the Corps. You're going to move up. With a few breaks, right to the top. I'm just now writing up my evaluation for your files. I plan to give you a very fine recommendation, Captain. Normally, I don't talk about this sort of thing, but I thought you might like to know."

"Thank you, sir," Captain Arnold said uneasily, opening his surface suit.

"Well, let's inspect the area, Captain."

The inspection was perfunctory. As he always did, the general paused at the pile monitor and watched, in the Dante screen, the virtually indescribable reactions being sustained far beneath the surface: molten rock flowing and smoking. Orange, blue and white flames danced as though in agony in the great, expanding cavern, danced and merged and vanished and reappeared in an ever-changing pattern.

Back at the locks, the general bid Captain Arnold good-by and turned to leave. Then, as if an afterthought came forward, he turned back.

"David, oh, David!"

"Yes, sir."

"Perhaps you remember a conversation we had a few weeks ago? I called on you for some technical advice." He held his helmet in his hands.

"When was that, sir?"

"Oh, it was about the technical feasibility of reversing the air-changing equipment, I believe. As you know, I can't be up on all the technical, purely detailed procedure, for all phases of the operation. That's what we have experts for." The last statement was unusually jovial. "I believe you told me, David, that the process was too far along at that time. Perhaps you remember?"

"General Shorter, when was that?"

"I thought you would remember, David. I'm sure it was you. Yes, I'm almost positive it was. But if you say. . . . Well, David, it wasn't quite so much as exactly a statement like that. But that was the general meaning of it, you know, stripped of all the technical language. You have to take it in the over-all context. That was the meaning I got." He laughed tactfully. "You're like lawyers, all you technicians. You answer everything yes and no at the same time. I hoped you'd remember the conversation. I got that idea from it." The general waited. "Well, David—don't look like that—it's not at all important. Just trying to refresh my own memory. It's not important, really. . . . Good night, David." He placed the helmet over his head.

"Good night, General."

Methodically the general completed his rounds. He laughed often and joked with the men and seemed in exceptionally good spirits.

Back in his own quarters, he brought out his diary. With a weary sigh, he sat down to it. He glanced at his timepiece. The day extended backward almost beyond memory but it was not yet late.

After thumbing the diary listlessly for several minutes—pausing now and then at a paragraph—he began to write. He put the events of the day down precisely in their logical sequence.

IV

The Committee took over the dining area when the general left for his tour of inspection. While the steward's department was preparing coffee for the interviewees, now assembling in the corridor, the four members of the Committee arranged themselves at the larger of the tables. Notepaper lay before them.

Mr. Tucker lighted a cigar and fingered it. "A rather good meal," he said.

The others nodded.

"I may as well start off, while we're waiting," Mr. Wallace said. "I'll summarize my somewhat contradictory observations.

"Superficially, the cultural level of the natives appeared quite primitive. The absence of tools would normally be indicative. On the other hand, the city was carved from rock in a way so as to suggest a very sophisticated technology. And writing, while apparently not practiced to any considerable extent, was known—

or, if not writing as we understand it, some advanced decorative technique. We've found two lines of it, at least.

"Again superficially, the city would suggest a nomadic tradition, but for its craftsmanship. It seems independent of any obvious supply of food and their equivalent of water, if any. Nor were any provisions in evidence for the disposal of waste products. Yet the city had the appearance of age and continual usage. If you notice, the floor of the recess was worn unevenly toward the center by what I should guess to be the traffic of several centuries.

"The thought naturally occurs that the aliens were the rather decadent relics of a highly developed technological civilization existing on the planet in the not too distant past. Yet Miracastle offers no evidence for the existence of a prior technology—no ruins, no residual radioactivity from atomic operations. In short, the city has no apparent genesis in the past.

"The alternative arises: perhaps the natives were not natives at all, but immigrants or colonists like ourselves. Yet the age of the city contradicts this.

"Perhaps there is a simple explanation, although it does not occur to me. But I do have this feeling. The city was utilitarian. To me, it calls to mind one of those exquisite etchings of Picasso. The severe economy of line suggests simplicity. Yet, on further inspection, you see that each line contributes to a rather bewildering variety of perspectives. I strongly suspect that the city and the people of Miracastle will remain one of the great, unsolved mysteries of the universe."

Mr. Wallace was finished with his remarks.

Mr. Ryan nodded. "Perhaps I'm deficient in sensibilities, but I find that the most . . . agonizing . . . thing of all is not ever to be able to know what these people were like. It's almost as if some part of us had been lopped off, isn't it? What did the people of Miracastle think about? What was their philosophy of life? What was their social organization? What was their ultimate goals? When you realize how much we learned of ourselves from an examination of our own primitive cultures, the sense of loss really comes home. Think how much more we could have learned of ourselves by acquiring the perspective of a truly alien culture.

It's almost as if we could really understand ourselves at last if we could only understand a totally alien culture . . ."

"Well, that's gone," Mr. Tucker said. The words were brittle and discrete. They hung in memory and the listeners waited as though for an echo of something shouted into a canyon. The echo did not come.

They were silent. Grief is the final knowledge of time. When one first learns that it can never be turned backward upon itself to permit the correction of past sins and the rightings of wrongs transfixed and forever unalterable. Grief is the frantic, futile beating of hands against a barrier without substance, both obscenely unreal and yet the only reality. Grief is the knowledge that we cannot step backwards before the death of loved ones and see those precious half-forgotten dream faces once again. Grief is the knowledge that time is immutable.

Outside the Richardson Dome, the wind was changing. It could now neither support the life that was nor the life that would be, and it howled in melancholy and insensate anguish its loneliness and longing to the eternal and ever-changing pattern of the stars.

The Committee concluded their interviews with an old-line corporal. He had just short of thirty years service and had several times traveled the two-way escalator of non-commissioned rank from master sergeant to private. He was perhaps typical of many of the older soldiers. His love of the Corps was expressed by his loyalty to it; his hatred of the Corps was expressed by his inability to abide by its regulations.

"You knew Sergeant Schuster very well?" Mr. Tucker asked.

"He was a new man," the corporal said. "He got on just before lift-off. A week, two weeks, something like that. I knew him, I guess. He was one of them kind that was always thinking. And like you know, sir, thinking ain't too good for a soldier. I've known a lot of guys like that in my time. You know what I mean? They're not cut out for the Corps."

"He talked to you quite a bit?"

The corporal turned to face Mr. Ryan. "He was always talking, sir. He was a regular nut. I thought for a while he was queer. He had all those crazy ideas."

"Like what, Corporal?"

"Oh, like—well, you know." The corporal hesitated and rummaged his memory without conspicuous success. "Sunsets," he said rather emphatically. "Talked about sunsets. Talked about just anything. Called me out back on Earth to look at a sunset once, I remember."

"What did he think about killing the natives?" Mr. Wallace asked.

The question alerted the mechanism which produced the almost-Pavlovian loyalty response.

"We didn't kill no natives," the corporal said. "They just died when we changed the air. Tough."

He looked at Mr. Wallace and then into the silence around him.

"Well . . . well, let's see. I guess you'd say that sort of got to him. I mean, you know, he thought it was—" the voice became distant, as though describing a fantastic event which he could not relate to anything in a rational environment—"he thought it was his fault. You know how some of these guys are. I used to have a platoon once, you know. And they say—" He twisted his mouth and changed his voice to a childish whine. "What for?" The voice reverted to normal. "They don't ask for any reason. They just ask. I say to them, I say, 'God damn it'—excuse me, sir—'I told you to do it, ain't that enough?' Well, this Schuster, sir, he worried all the time. He got so he cut himself shaving. Damnedest thing. Oh, hell, maybe for the last week, every morning, he came out a bloody mess. Patches of toilet paper all over his face. 'I can't shave,' he'd say. 'My God, I can't shave.' He wasn't nervous, either. His hands were okay. They didn't shake. It's just that he couldn't shave. Like I say, he was a nut."

No one spoke for a moment, and the corporal twisted uncomfortably.

Then Mr. Tucker said, "Well, Corporal, tell me this, please."

"Yes, sir."

"What's your own personal impression of General Shorter?"

"The old man?" the corporal asked in surprise. "He's okay."

"Feel free to discuss this," Mr. Flison said. "We'd like to know, really, what your opinion is."

"Like I say, he's okay. He's got a job to do. You know, he busted me once. General Shorter personally, I mean. Hell, I don't hold it against him, though. He's got his job to do, I got mine. I wouldn't say anything against General Shorter, no, sir. He's a soldier. I mean, you know . . . he's a soldier."

After the corporal was dismissed, Mr. Tucker said, "Well, gentlemen, I guess we've about wrapped it up here. I think this is enough. Anybody's mind changed? I don't think we need any more, do you?"

Mr. Wallace sighed heavily. He looked down at his hands.

General Shorter was still at his writing desk when he was notified that Mr. Tucker would like to see him first thing in the morning.

"Another day of it, eh?" the general asked the sergeant who brought the message.

"No, sir. From the other crew, I hear they're planning to leave tomorrow."

The general's face relaxed. His smile reflected weary tolerance. "Had enough in one day, have they? It's about time they let us get back to work."

After the sergeant left, the general wrote a final paragraph:

"I've just been informed the 'investigation' is completed. In record time, it seems. They finished up in the mess tonight, talking to some of the men. So what did it all really accomplish? They took a long ship that could better have been used somewhere else. Half my men are down with the virus. They almost cost me my schedule. And to what end? Just another piece of paper somewhere. Put Miracastle on the scale against some nice, heavy report and see which way the scale tips."

The general closed the diary. It was late now. He was very tired.

Mr. Tucker, after breakfast, knocked on the general's door.

"Come in," General Shorter called.

The civilian entered. The general dismissed the orderly with a nod. "And I'll need some clean towels for tonight," he called. His voice was hoarse.

"Yes, sir."

The door closed. The two of them were alone.

"Sit down. Excuse the cold. Got it last night. What do you say to a brandy?"

"Don't let me stop you."

"I never drink alone."

"Perhaps you'd better," Mr. Tucker said.

The general had paused just short of the cupboard. He turned slowly. "In that case, I'll make an exception, this once." He poured. "Just what did you mean by that, sir? Let's get to the point."

"General Shorter, we're going to have to ask you to come back with us."

The general bent slightly forward. His lips were partly open, as though he were listening to hear a second time.

"Why," he said, "I've too much work to do, sir. I'm afraid that's out of the question. It's just not possible at all."

Mr. Tucker waited.

General Shorter poured himself another brandy. His back was to the civilian.

"There's nothing more important, right now, than my job here," he said. He drank the brandy in a single gulp.

"I don't see how it can wait, General," Mr. Tucker said.

The general's lips were dry. He closed his eyes tightly for a moment against the alcohol and the cold. He licked his lips. "What's the formal charge?"

Mr. Tucker bent forward. His voice was soft and curious, as though the question were his final effort to understand something that puzzled him for a long time. "What do you think it is, General?"

"What could it be?" the general said sharply. "I follow orders, sir. I was sent out here to make this planet suitable for human habitation. This is exactly what I have been doing." His voice was growing progressively more angry and with an effort he curbed himself. "Put yourself in my position. I did what any field commander would have done. It was too late to stop it. I've got—It's a question of the limits of normal prudence. A matter of interpretation, sir."

The general was in the process of pouring still another drink. The slender brandy glass broke under the force of his anger. He opened his palm. Blood trickled from between his fingers.

The general looked up from the hand and fleeting annoyance came and went before he was recalled to present reality. His eyes met Mr. Tucker's.

Mr. Tucker suddenly shivered as if touched by a wind from beyond the most distant stars, a wind which whispered: The aliens are among us.

"General," Mr. Tucker said, "the formal charge is murder."

NEW APPLES IN THE GARDEN

Eddie Hibbs reported for work and was almost immediately called out on an emergency. It was the third morning in succession for emergencies.

This time a section of distribution cable had blown in West Los Angeles. Blown cable was routine, but each instance merited the attention of an assistant underground supervisor.

Eddie climbed down the manhole with the foreman of the maintenance crew. There were deep pull marks on the lead sheath above where the cable had blown.

"Where'd they get it?" he asked.

"It came in from a job on the East Side."

"Sloppy work," Eddie said. "Water got in the splice?"

"These new guys. . . ." the foreman said.

Eddie fingered the pull marks. "I think she's about shot anyway. How much is like this?"

"A couple of hundred feet."

"All this bad?"

"Yep."

Eddie whistled. "About fifteen thousand dollars worth. Well. Cut her back to here and make splices. Stand over them while they do it."

"I'll need two men for a week."

"I'll try to find them for you. Send through the paper."

"I can probably find maybe another thousand miles or so that's about this bad."

"Don't bother," Eddie said.

That was Eddie's productive work during the morning. With traffic and two sections of street torn up by the water people, he did not get back to his office until just before lunch. He listened to the Stock Market reports while he drove.

He learned that spiraling costs had retarded the modernization program of General Electronics and much of their present equipment was obsolete in terms of current price factors. He was also told to anticipate that declining sales would lead to declining production, thereby perpetuating an unfortunate cycle. And finally he was warned that General Electronics was an example of the pitfalls involved in investing in the so-called High Growth stocks.

Eddie turned off the radio in the parking lot as the closing Dow-Jones' report was starting.

During lunch, he succeeded in reading two articles in a six-week-old issue of Electrical World, the only one of the dozen technical journals he found time for now.

At 12:35 word filtered into the department that one of the maintenance crew, Ramon Lopez, had been killed. A forty-foot ladder broke while atop it Lopez was hosing down a pothead, and he was driven backward into the concrete pavement by the high-pressure water.

Eddie tried to identify the man. The name was distantly familiar but there was no face to go with it. Finally the face came. He smoked two cigarettes in succession. He stubbed the last one out angrily.

"That was a tough one," his supervisor, Forester, said, sitting on the side of Eddie's desk. Normally exuberant, he was left melancholy and distracted by the accident. "You know the guy?"

"To speak to."

"Good man."

"After I thought about it a little bit," Eddie said, "I remembered he was transferring tomorrow. Something like this brings a man up short, doesn't it?"

"A hell of a shame. Just a hell of a shame."

They were silent for a minute.

"How was the market this morning?" Forester asked.

"Up again. I didn't catch the closing averages."

"I guess that makes a new high."

"Third straight day," Eddie said.

"Hell of a shame," Forester said.

"Yeah, Lopez was a nice guy."

"Well...." Forester's voice trailed off in embarrassment.

"Yeah, well...."

"I wanted to remind you about the budget meeting."

Eddie glanced at his watch. "Hour and a half?"

"Yeah. You know, I feel like . . . never mind. What about the burial transformers, you get on it yet?"

"The ones we're running in the water mains for cooling? They're out of warranty. None of the local shops can rewind them until the manufacturer sends out a field engineer to set them up for the encapsulation process."

"How long is that going to take?" Forester asked.

"They tell me several months. Still doesn't leave us with anything. The plant says they've fixed the trouble, but between them and the rewind shop, they can buck it back and forth forever."

"I guess we'll have to go back to the pad-mounted type."

"People with the Gold Medallion Homes aren't going to like the pads by their barbecues."

Forester uncoiled a leg. "Draw up a memorandum on it, will you, Eddie?" He stood up. "That thing sure got me today. There's just entirely too many of these accidents. A ladder breaking. I don't know."

Eddie tried to find something intelligent to say. Finally he said, "It was a rough one, all right."

After Forester left, Eddie picked up, listlessly from the top of the stack one of the preliminary reports submitted for his approval.

The report dealt with three thousand capacitors purchased last year from an Eastern firm, now bankrupt. The capacitors were beginning to leak. Eddie called the electrical laboratory to see what progress was being made on the problem.

The supervisor refreshed his memory from the records. He reported: "I don't have any adhesive man to work on it. Purchasing has half a dozen suppliers lined up—but none have any test data. I don't know when we'll get the time. We're on a priority program checking out these new, low-cost terminations."

"Can't we certify the adhesive to some AIEE spec or something?" Eddie asked.

"I don't know of any for sealing capacitors, Eddie. Not on the maintenance end, at least."

"Maybe Purchasing can get a guarantee from one of the suppliers?"

"For the hundred dollars of compound that's involved? What good would that do us?"

Eddie thanked him and hung up. He signed the preliminary report.

He turned to the next one.

At 2:30 Forester came by and the two of them made their way between the jig-saw projections of maple and mahogany to the Conference Room.

Fourteen men were involved in the conference, all from operating departments. They shuffled in over a five minute period, found seats, lit cigarettes, talked and joked with one another.

When one of the assistants to the manager came in, they fell silent.

"Gentlemen," he said, "I think I'd better get right to the point today. The Construction Program in the Valley has now used up two bond issues. The voters aren't going to approve a third one."

He paused for effect then continued briskly:

"I see by the morning's Times that the mayor is appointing a watch-dog commission. I guess you all saw it, too. The Department of Water and Power of the City of Los Angeles is going to be badly—and I mean badly—in the red at the end of the fiscal year.

"We're in hot water.

"We do not seem to be getting through to the operating departments regarding the necessity for cost reduction. I have here last month's breakdown on the Bunker Hill substation 115 KV installation. Most of you have seen it already, I think. I had it sent around. Now—"

The analysis continued for some ten minutes to conclude with an explosion:

"We've got to impose a ten per cent across the board cut on operating expenses."

One of the listeners, more alert than the rest, asked, "That go for salaries?"

"For personnel making more than eight hundred dollars a

month it does."

There was a moment of shocked silence.

"You can't make that stick," one of the supervisors said. "Half my best men will be out tomorrow looking for better offers— and finding them, too."

"I'm just passing on what I was told."

The men in the room shuffled and muttered under their breaths.

"O.K., that's the way they want it," one of the supervisors said.

"I've brought along the notices for the affected personnel. Please see they're distributed when you leave."

After the meeting, Forester walked with Eddie back to his desk.

"You be in tomorrow, Eddie?"

"I guess I will, Les. I really don't know, yet."

"I'd hate to lose you."

"It's going to make it pretty rough. A man's fixed expenses don't come down."

"I'll see what I can do for you, maybe upgrade the classification—"

"Thanks, Les."

Back at his desk, Eddie looked at his watch. Nearly time for the Safety Meeting. Lost-time injuries had been climbing for the last four months.

While waiting, he signed a sixty-three page preliminary report recommending a program for the orderly replacement of all transmission and distribution cable installed prior to 1946. It was estimated that the savings, in the long run, would total some quarter of a billion dollars. The initial expense, however, was astronomical.

After the Safety Meeting, Eddie prepared another memorandum indicating the acute need for a better training program and an increase in maintenance personnel. Shortage of qualified technicians was chronic.

At four twenty-five, the night supervisor phoned in to say he was having engine trouble with his new car and would be delayed until about six o'clock. Eddie agreed to wait for him.

Eddie dialed home to let his wife, Lois, know he would be late again. A modulated low-frequency note told him the home phone was out of order.

Ray Morely, one of the night-shift engineers, came in with coffee. "You still here, Eddie?"

"Yeah, until Wheeler makes it. His car's down."

"Market hit a new high."

"Yeah. I guess you heard about the meeting today?"

Ray sipped coffee. "Budget again? I missed the day crew. I got hung up in traffic and was a little late."

"A pay cut goes with it, this time."

"You're kidding?"

"Been by your desk yet?"

"No."

"I'm not kidding. Ten per cent for those making above eight hundred."

"Nobody's going to put up with that," Ray said. "We're in an engineering shortage. We've got ICBMs rusting in their silos all over the country because we can't afford the engineering maintenance—that's how bad it is. Everybody'll quit."

"I don't think they'll make it stick. Ramon Lopez, one of the truck crew, was killed today hosing down a high-voltage pothead."

"No kidding?"

Eddie told him about the accident.

"That was a rough one to lose, wasn't it?"

The phone rang.

Ray said, "I'll get it."

He listened for a minute and hung up. "There's an outage in the Silver Lake Area. The brakes on a bus failed and took out an overhead section."

Eddie sat back. "No sense in you going. With work traffic on the surface streets until the freeway gets fixed, they won't get the truck there until 6:30 or so."

"Right." Ray drank coffee reflectively. "You going looking?"

"I'm an old-timer. I got a lot of seniority. How about you?"

"I got bills. It's going to cost me near a hundred a month—

that's a steep bite."

"I still think they'll back off."

"They'll have to," Ray said. "If not right now, when the pressure gets on. You ask me, we've got them by the short hair." He settled into the chair. "I see it as an organic phenomenon. When society gets as complex as ours, it has to grow more and more engineers. But there's a feedback circuit in effect. The more engineers we grow, the more complex society becomes. Each new one creates the need for two more. I get a sort of feeling of—I don't know—vitality, I guess, when I walk into, say, an automated factory. All that machinery and all that electronic gear is like a single cell in a living organism—an organism that's growing every day, multiplying like bacteria. And it's always sick, and we're the doctors. That's job security. We're riding the wave of the future. I don't think they'll make a salary cut stick."

"I hope you're right," Eddie said.

Eddie checked out at 7:15, when the night supervisor finally arrived. As he left the building, he noted that a burglar alarm down the street had gone off, probably because of a short circuit. The clanking set his nerves on edge. Apprehensively he felt a rising wind against his cheeks.

At home, he was greeted with a perfunctory kiss at the door.

"Honey," Lois told him, "you took the check book, and I didn't have any money."

"Something come up? I'm sorry."

"We're all out of milk. The milk man didn't come today. Their homogenizing machinery broke down. I phoned the dairy about nine; and then, of course, the phone has been on the blink since about eleven or a little before, so I couldn't ask you to bring some home."

"I kept trying to get you."

"I figured you had to work late again, when you weren't here at six, and I knew you'd be here when you got here."

Eddie sat down and she sat on the chair arm beside him. "How did it go today?"

He started to tell her about the wage cut and Ramon Lopez; but then he didn't want to talk about it. "So-so," he said. "There was an outage over in the Silver Lake Area just before I left."

"Fixed yet?"

"I doubt it," he said. "Probably a couple of more hours."

"Gee," she said, "when I think of all that meat in the deep freezer...."

"I wouldn't stock so much," he said. "I really wouldn't."

She twisted away from him. "Honey. I'm jittery. Something's . . . I don't know. In the air, I guess."

The wind rattled the windows.

While Lois was warming dinner, his son came in.

"Hi, Eddie."

"Hi, Larry."

"Eddie, when we gonna get the TV fixed?"

Eddie put down the newspaper. "We just don't have a hundred dollars or so right now." He searched for matches on the table by the chair. "Lois, oh, Lois, where're the matches?"

She came in. "They were all out Friday at the store, and I keep forgetting to lay in a supply. Use my lighter over there."

"About the TV—"

Lois was wiping her hands on the paper towel she had brought with her. "Replacement parts are hard to find for the older sets," she said. "Anyway. I read today Channel Three finally went off the air. That leaves only Two and Seven. And the programs aren't any good, now, are they? All those commercials and all?"

"They do use a lot of old stuff I've already seen," the son admitted, "but every once in a while there's something new."

"Let's talk about it some other time, Larry, O.K.?" Eddie said. "How's that? It's almost your bed-time. Studies done?"

"All but the Library report."

"Well, finish it, and—"

"I got to read the book down there. Two classes assigned it and they don't have the copies to let us check out. And I want to ask you about something, Eddie."

"Daddy's tired. His dinner's on. Come on, Eddie. I'll set it right now. And Larry, you've already eaten. . . ."

After dinner, Eddie got back to the paper, the evening Times. It was down to eight pages, mostly advertising. There was a front-page editorial reluctantly announcing a price increase.

"They raise the price once more, and we'll just quit taking it," Lois said. "You read about the airplane crash in Florida? Wasn't that terrible? What do you think caused it?"

"Metal fatigue, probably," Eddie said. "It was a twenty-year-old jet."

"The company said it wasn't that at all."

"They always do," Eddie said.

"I don't guess the payroll check came today or you'd have mentioned it."

"Payroll's still all balled up. Somebody pressed a wrong button on the new machine and some fifty thousand uncoded cards got scattered all over the office."

"Oh, no! What do the poor people, who don't have bank accounts, do?"

"Just wait, like we wait."

"You had a bad day," Lois said. "I can tell."

"No. . . ." Eddie said. "Not really, I guess."

"Still working on Saturday?"

"I guess so. Nothing was said. Maybe it'll get easier after the end of the month."

"You said it was all that new construction work in the Valley that's making you so shorthanded."

"That's part of it."

"They're not scheduled to finish until . . . when, sometime next year, isn't it?"

"The end of '81 right now."

"Eddie! Listen to me! I hardly ever see you any more. You're not going to have to put in all this overtime for the next two years!"

"Of course not," Eddie said. "Maybe after this month, that's all, and the work load will level off."

Larry, dressed for bed, came in. "Eddie?"

"Your father's tired."

"I want to ask him something."

"What is it, Larry?" Eddie asked.

"Eddie, you know the little culture I was running for science class? Something's wrong. Will you look at it?"

"Daddy's. . . ."

"I'll look at it, Lois." Eddie accompanied his son to his son's room.

"What do you think is wrong, Dad?"

"Well, let's see. . . ."

"What is it?" Larry asked. "What made it stop growing?"

Eddie did not answer for a minute. Then: "You start with one or two . . . well, it's like this, Larry. I'm afraid it's dead. They grow exponentially. Figure out how much money you'd have at the end of a month if you started with just a penny and doubled your money every day. In just a little while, you'd have all the money in the world. Figure it out sometime. Things that grow exponentially, they just don't know when to quit. And your culture, here, it grew until the environment could no longer support it and all at once the food was eaten up and it died."

"I . . . see. . . . Something like that could just grow until it took over the whole world, couldn't it?"

Again Eddie was silent for a moment. Then he rumpled his son's hair. "That's science fiction, Larry."

Later, while they were listening to FM, there was a news break reporting a fire out of control in South Los Angeles.

"That's near Becky's, I'll bet," she said. "I better phone."

The phone was still out of order.

"I sure feel cut off without a phone."

After an interlude of music, Lois said, "Larry wants to be an engineer, now. I guess after what you said, maybe that's a pretty good thing."

Eddie looked up from his cigarette. "Why this all of a sudden?"

"One of his teachers told him what you said—there's a growing engineering shortage."

"I thought he wanted to be an astronaut."

"You know Larry. That was last week. His teacher said we're not going to start up the space program again. It's too expensive. We just don't have the technical man-power and materials to spare."

"We are in. . . . But these kids, young kids they're turning out—they aren't getting the education today. And if anything, I sometimes think it almost makes our jobs even worse, correcting their mistakes. I sometimes wonder where it's all going to stop."

There was more news from the fire front.

Fire fighters were having a very difficult time. Two water mains had broken and the pressure was dropping. The fire was reported to have been caused by the explosion of a gas main. Rising winds did not promise to abate until dawn.

"I sure wish I could get through to Beck," Lois said. "Oh, I guess I told you, did I? Her sister has hypoglycemia, they found out. That's why she's been tired all the time."

"Never heard of it."

"Low blood sugar. It's caused by an overactive gland on the pancreas. And treatment is just the opposite of what you'd think, too. I'll bet you'd never guess. If you increase the amount of sugar in the diet, the gland becomes just that much more active to get rid of it and the hypoglycemia gets worse. It's what I'll bet you engineers call a feedback. Isn't that what you call it? Well . . . the way doctors treat it is to reduce the amount of sugar you eat. And after a little bit, the pancreas gets back its normal function, and the patient gets well. I told you you'd never guess!"

After a long time, Eddie said, very softly, "Oh."

Just after midnight, they went to bed.

"I've been . . ." Lois began and then stopped. "I don't know. Jumpy. The market was up again today. Another all-time high. Do you think there'll be another Crash? Like 'way back in 1929."

She could feel him lying tense beside her in the darkness. "No," he said slowly, "I don't think so. I don't think there'll be a Crash."

In spite of the warmth of the room, she could not suppress an involuntary shudder whose cause was nameless. Suddenly, she did not want to ask any more questions.

The wind was rattling the windows.

www.ingramcontent.com/pod-product-compliance
Lightning Source LLC
Chambersburg PA
CBHW020651180626
46816CB00003B/1221